magic of the
moonlight

ALSO BY ELLEN SCHREIBER

ELLEN SCHREIBER

magic of the
moonlight

a full moon novel

KATHERINE TEGEN BOOKS
An Imprint of HarperCollins Publishers

To my mom and my husband, with all my love

HarperTeen is an imprint of HarperCollins Publishers.
Katherine Tegen Books is an imprint of HarperCollins Publishers.

Magic of the Moonlight
Copyright © 2012 by Ellen Schreiber

Library of Congress Cataloging-in-Publication Data is available.
ISBN 978-0-06-198657-4 (trade bdg.)

Typography by Amy Ryan
12 13 14 15 16 LP/RRDH 10 9 8 7 6 5 4 3 2 1
❖
First Edition

CONTENTS

"Beware of a bite under a full moon.
It will complicate your love life."
—Dr. Camille Meadows

ONE

a werewolf among us

It was official. I was in love with a werewolf.

As extraordinary as that sounded, I was coming to terms with the fact that my heart and soul had been taken by Brandon Maddox. He was a hot and handsome Westsider in a town that favored the east, and under the glow of a full moon he would turn into a creature of the moonlight.

It was several days since I'd first kissed Brandon in his werewolf form. The kiss was breathtaking and magical and I couldn't think of anything else. The March weather was still cool and crisp, and I was heading from the school library over to the gym after school to meet my best friends, Ivy and Abby, who were watching their boyfriends, Dylan and Jake, and my former boyfriend, Nash, at basketball practice. I must have been smiling, still thinking about Brandon's lips, when

I caught up to the girls sitting on the bleachers.

"You are back together!" Ivy said. "For good this time!"

"Back together with who?" I asked. "I'm not sure what you mean."

Ivy pulled a face. "Don't be sneaky. With Nash, silly!"

The whistle blew and the guys headed to the fountain for water.

I thought this was the perfect time to confess to my closest friends about my relationship with Brandon. I hadn't told them before for several reasons. One, he was from the wrong side of town and, therefore, an outsider, and two, they thought it was cool that we three best friends were dating guys who were also best friends. And since I had crushed out on Nash for a long time, I knew I'd been lucky to go out with him. The only problem was that there was something missing between us, and that something—love—I'd seemed to find with Brandon Maddox.

Since Brandon had found Abby's missing dog, an act that had obviously gotten him on Abby's good side, I was hoping my friends might be receptive to my confession about dating the transfer student. Ready to break the news, I leaned in close to my friends when two strong hands grabbed my shoulders. I noticed a familiar class ring glistening against my pale pink sweater. It was the ring my former boyfriend Nash had worn since freshman year—the one he recently tried to give me, and the one I had seen on the hand holding a flashlight when I was in the woods with Brandon as he changed into a werewolf.

"And here he is," Ivy said as the guys joined us on the bleachers. "Your boyfriend."

"I was telling them before practice about how we got back together," Nash said, scooting in next to me, hot and sweaty from practice. "Officially."

Nash was gorgeous. His chin was rugged and his perfect complexion radiated. His sandy hair was messy in a good way. He had the kind of smile that made a girl want to kiss him, and eyes that let on that many had.

"But that's not—" I began, but Nash put his finger over my lips.

"I was telling them that you saw the error of your ways," he said smoothly. "And under the moonlight, with the full moon glowing, that something changed drastically." He shot me an all-knowing glance.

"So now we'll continue to be a happy sixsome," Ivy said. "Forever."

My stomach turned. I wanted to tell Ivy that I was in love with Brandon. But with Nash alluding to Brandon's changing into a werewolf, it would have to wait. It was one thing to get them to accept me dating a Westsider, but I couldn't imagine what they'd say to my dating a werewolf. We grabbed our things, and the guys began escorting us to the gymnasium exit.

I hung back and signaled Nash to do the same. Ivy and Abby winked as if they expected I was requesting canoodling time from him.

"This is how you want us to get back together?" I asked quietly when the rest were out of earshot. "By extorting me? You'll tell them about Brandon if I don't pretend you and I have reunited?"

"It's for your own safety," he said. "You know what I saw. As if it's not enough that he's from the Westside—I saw what happened!"

"You don't know what you're talking about," I said.

"I was there, Celeste. I'm doing this for your own good. A werewolf in this town wouldn't go over very well. I could have him locked up in a nuthouse."

"Shh!" I scolded. "He's not a nut!"

"There is something wrong with that dude! I can't believe you like him," he said fervently. Then his eyes softened. "I can't stand by and watch you hanging out with a monster, Celeste. What would you do in my situation? I don't want him to hurt you. Don't you understand?"

Nash's tone was sincere and his true caring warmed my heart. I knew that I'd be concerned, too, if I saw someone I had affection for standing next to a werewolf. Nash having this compassion made me feel good, but he was going about it in the wrong way.

"Brandon is a great guy," I said. "No one needs to protect me from him."

Nash's lips tensed. "Listen—I was there." He faced me squarely, his brow furrowed in anger. "I saw what happened. He's not normal, Celeste. You have to know that." Nash was adamant in trying to convince me. "He is dangerous."

"That's not true. He's really just the opposite."

"He's an animal. I saw it for myself."

Nash was such a hypocrite sometimes. "Then why did you run?" I asked. "If you were so afraid for me, why did you take off and leave me alone with him?" I started off for my friends when he caught up to me.

"I'm here now," he said softly. His declaration was very enticing. Nash wasn't angry anymore, but instead I could see fear in his eyes at the path I was choosing. He was caring and concerned for real. Beyond a guy trying to get a girl—but in this case a friend trying to help a friend. "I'm not leaving until you promise not to see him." Nash wasn't bullying me. He was instead talking to me like a friend or a big brother. I was touched by his concern but struggled with him asking me to abandon Brandon, the one I loved.

"I can't," I said.

Nash folded his arms in disgust. "Then I have no choice." He headed off to catch up with our clique.

This time I caught up to him and faced him squarely. "You are my friend, Nash," I said, feeling short of breath. "Why are you doing this to me?"

"Because I am your friend. And friends look out for each other."

"Not like this. If you plan to extort me," I countered, "then I'll go ahead and tell them I'm dating Brandon now myself." I began to march over toward Ivy and Abby when I felt my backpack tugged and I was stopped in my tracks.

Nash glared at me with vengeance. "Then you are forcing me to do something I wasn't going to do," he said boldly. "I'm going to tell them what I saw. Brandon changed into a freaking were—"

"Shh!" I said, waving my hand in front of his mouth.

My friends were waiting by the gym door. I imagined Nash storming over to them and dropping the bombshell on them.

Dating Brandon wasn't something I'd be able to deny. I was lousy at lying. For one thing, I had an ultrastrong conscience, and two, my face would flush and my upper lip would quiver, immediately giving me away. It might be hard for my friends to be convinced that Brandon was a real werewolf, but they wouldn't be able to get over my dating him for the past few months and not telling them myself.

"Give me a little more time," I said to Nash.

I knew I wasn't about to stop dating Brandon and start seeing Nash again, but I had to buy myself more time before Nash told everyone Brandon was a werewolf.

The handsome jock smiled winningly. "I'll show you how things will be different," he said genuinely. "How they should have been all along."

For a moment, I wondered what it would be like if Nash changed. I imagined him helping decorate the halls at Pine Tree Village Retirement Community, walking in Willow Park together under the moonlight, or arriving at my home with a bouquet of flowers. It would have been what I'd wanted from Nash if he was up for the change, but his romantic declarations had come too late.

I raced over to Ivy and Abby and opened the gym door. We could see the main entrance and parking lot. The guys, still hot from their practice game, embraced the chilly air.

If anyone was going to tell Ivy and Abby about my seeing Brandon, it was going to be me. And I didn't want anyone knowing about his transformation.

Brandon had unknowingly forced Nash to become the person I'd wanted Nash to be several months ago. If Nash had paid this much attention to me when we were dating, I'd never have been interested in anyone else. But his romantic behavior was happening a full moon too late. I knew it would be easier to take the road with the basketball player than the one with the werewolf, but I had to be true to myself. I was captivated, compelled, and perhaps under a spell. But whatever that spell was, it had the face of Brandon, by day or by full moonlight.

"Look!" Ivy said, pointing to Brandon's Jeep. A wig and costume were lying on the hood of his truck. On the driver's-side door was painted the word WOLFMAN. "Brandon was that werewolf all along," Ivy continued, referring to a masked werewolf that had been terrorizing the town. In fact, that phony werewolf had been Nash, but no one else except me knew who the werewolf had really been.

I looked at Nash, who shrugged his shoulders. "I'm not a

vandal," he said defensively.

"Brandon was the werewolf?" Abby said. "That's odd. He always sits in the back of class so quietly. He doesn't seem the type to run around town for attention."

"But remember when he stood by the classroom window when the wolves came to school and he psychically made them run off?" Jake said. "Pretty freaky!"

"Maybe he really is a wolfman," Ivy teased.

"I guess he was playing a joke on us," Dylan said. "Moving to this new town—maybe he thinks we are fools."

"You think he was the one playing tricks?" Nash asked us all. It was as if he was longing to tell them his secret, too.

"We didn't have any werewolf spottings until he came here," Ivy pointed out.

"And he did put that Vulcan mind meld on those wolves at school," Jake stressed again.

"I'm not so sure," Abby said. "It seems too convenient that he'd just put the costume on his own car. Why would he do that?"

"Why do you think he wouldn't?" Dylan said, almost challenging. "I don't know why you are defending him. He's the one who jumped out at you in that stupid outfit and scared the life out of you."

"I'm not. It just doesn't make sense."

"Well, why would he run around town dressed as a werewolf in the first place?" Ivy posed. "A cry for help? He wears those fingerless gloves. He eats like a pig. He's weird. But the good news is it's over now. We're all safe. I'm really glad to know it was just a lame joke."

"But it still surprises me that he'd be the one to jump out at me like he did," Abby said. "He's usually so quiet in school."

"Well, at least we don't have a werewolf running around Legend's Run anymore," Ivy said.

"Or do we?" Jake growled, and tickled her tiny waist.

"Yes, it's over now," Nash said, glaring at me.

This was the moment. I couldn't watch Brandon be a punch line to the students' very unpractical jokes anymore. I needed to declare my love for Brandon. And if Nash decided to tell them what he saw, then so be it. I'd tell them he was pranking them and see whose story was more believable.

I looked intently at my friends. "I have something to tell you," I said bravely.

Just then I caught sight of Brandon walking to his Jeep. His dark hair flopped with his long and sexy stride. He stopped suddenly when he spotted the werewolf costume lying on the hood. He glanced around and then noticed us standing outside the gymnasium. He seemed to be staring right at me; his gaze lingered. I felt his disappointment, and I was deeply saddened.

He picked up the costume and tossed it in a nearby garbage can.

Even from my vantage point, I could sense his pain and disgust. He knew who had been wearing the costume—the handsome guy standing beside me.

I lurched forward to go to Brandon, but Nash grabbed my wrist. His grip was strong; I couldn't have wiggled free if my life depended on it. My heart raced, seeing Brandon there—having to fight against the moonlight and the sunlight—alone. His loneliness was palpable to me. He was so gorgeous—he should be the star of Legend's Run High School instead of the misfit.

Was this going to be my life? Hopelessly in love with a guy who was a werewolf, and not able to be with him at school because of my friends? And was Nash going to make me keep my relationship from them so he wouldn't reveal Brandon's lycan secret?

I contemplated my own integrity. I didn't want to melt under peer pressure, but losing all of my friends and making Brandon's life here at Legend's Run even lonelier made this a difficult decision. I was always the rational person, the problem solver who laid out all her options before jumping into anything difficult.

However, there had been one time in my life when I didn't heed warnings or act thoughtfully instead of emotionally—that moment when the full moon was bursting and I was dying to kiss Brandon Maddox.

Brandon had changed into a werewolf, but I had changed, too. And I wasn't sure who I was becoming. Stuck in the middle of two good things—both with major downsides. As if high school wasn't challenging enough.

"We've got to go," Dylan said, giving Abby a good-bye smooch.

"Thanks for hanging out," Jake said to Ivy.

She kissed him and gave him a tight squeeze.

Nash lingered for a moment. I think he sensed I wasn't about to kiss him, so he just said, "Remember what we talked about," and started back to the gymnasium.

We girls huddled together and made our way to our cars.

"Let's all go to the mall," Ivy said. "We can grab some pizza at the food court."

"Maybe I'll catch up to you guys later." I couldn't think of eating—my stomach still felt pained having watched Brandon being harassed. "I've got a few things I have to do."

"What could be more important than being with us?" Ivy asked as she got into her SUV.

"Only one thing," I mumbled under my breath. I jumped into my car and headed straight for Brandon's.

When I got to Brandon's grandparents' house, I found him outside his guesthouse, crouching down by his Jeep with a hose, a bucketful of soapy water, and a rag. He was beginning to wipe off the word *WOLFMAN* from the side of his Jeep.

I didn't know what to say. I wasn't sure how Brandon would react to me.

He spotted me, and for a moment I sensed his pain. I knew he loved that Jeep and took great care of it. I also knew that it must be horrible to have your property and name defamed in front of the entire school.

However, his royal blue eyes bore through me, and I saw a hint of a smile. I felt the sadness wash away and was exhilarated in his presence.

"I can help you with that," I said, walking to him.

"No, that's okay," he said, standing up. "It needed to be washed anyway."

I took the rag from his hand and began to wash away the letter *W*. The paint was pretty thick, and it took some muscle to get rid of it.

"Fortunately the morons didn't use spray paint," he said. "It's just like paint you'd find in art class."

"Nash didn't do this," I said. "He might have left the costume there—he's a prankster—but not a vandal."

"So? Why should that make me feel better?" He took the rag from me and began washing it himself.

"I didn't mean to defend him. I just wanted you to know."

He didn't respond but kept on scrubbing.

"I want to tell them," I began. "I want to tell my friends how I feel about you."

Brandon was surprised. He wiped his hands off with a dry rag. "About us?"

"Yes," I said. "And if they don't like it, then they're not true friends, right?"

"Well, I can see Nash not liking it."

I cracked a smile then, too.

He took my sudsy hands and began to dry them with the

rag. It was relaxing as he attended to me by rubbing my hands with the cloth, and I stared blissfully up at his gorgeous face.

"And Ivy," he said. "She seems possessive of you. And I don't fit neatly into her world."

It would be hard—our clique was strong, and no one had penetrated it for years. If she knew I was seeing Brandon instead of Nash, she'd be bummed, to say the least. I imagined Ivy and Abby snubbing me in class, whispering together when I walked in the hallway, filling in my seat at lunch with their backpacks. No calls, texts, or study buddies. I was afraid I'd lose my best friends.

But it wasn't going to make me happy to lose Brandon, either.

"I'm ready to tell them," I said. "That is . . . if you want this, too."

"Yeah," he said. "I do."

He tossed the rag into the bucket, took my hands again, and drew me to him. A few soap bubbles from his sleeve tickled my cheek as he caressed my face. My boots splashed in the sudsy puddles.

"So, you'll sit with me at lunch?" he said dreamily.

"Or you'll sit with me."

It was going to be different. I'd sat with Ivy since elementary school. I knew it would be difficult to stare at her from across the lunchroom and watch her and Abby giggling and gossiping without me. But if it was too awkward with Brandon and me at our table, we'd have to eat at his.

"And we'll meet each other after class," I said.

"I wouldn't want to meet anyone else," he replied with an extra squeeze.

I imagined getting smirks as we passed other Eastsiders in the hallways. And who knows, the Westsiders might not be too happy, either. There would be obstacles, but to be in the company of the guy I was in love with, I was ready.

But then I remembered that night Nash saw Brandon change into a werewolf. And I thought about how Nash had threatened to tell my friends what he'd witnessed if I continued to see Brandon.

"But there is one problem," I said.

"What do you mean?"

"Nash threatened me—he said that if I continue dating you, he'll tell the whole school what he saw that night—you changing into a werewolf."

"What? Are you kidding me?"

"He's genuinely concerned for me," I confessed. "I can't blame him for that."

Brandon appeared sullen. "I know . . . I'd be the same if I saw what he saw."

"But I tried to convince him it wasn't as bad as he thought. That you aren't dangerous."

"I'm sure he believed that," he said, kicking the dirt.

"But what if he tells someone?" I asked.

"Who will believe him?" he wondered. "He doesn't have proof."

"I'm hoping that everyone will think he's pranking them again and they won't listen. But you're already being called Wolfman and had your Jeep vandalized. I'm not sure what those vandals might do next. People love to pick on someone—and now you are the target. This could make it worse."

"It's okay. I can handle it," he said.

I was pleased with his reaction, but I wanted him to have full disclosure of what the challenges might be. "I know you can. But Nash is competitive," I said. "It's in his nature to fight. I'm afraid he'll go for the jugular."

Brandon thought. "I'm not going to let him dictate my life."

I was proud of Brandon's bravery, and even though I was hoping everyone would see Nash's declaration as a joke, I wasn't convinced it would be okay. The more I thought about it, the more I worried.

"But . . ." I started, "when the next full moon comes out, do you think everyone will be looking for you?"

He thought again, this time taking a moment. "Yes, they will."

Now I was really worried. It was one thing to be teased, another to be hunted.

"I can't do that to you," I said. "Just to have what I want. It's not fair to you."

"But then it's not fair to you, either. To have to walk through the halls on the arm of a guy they are calling a werewolf."

Brandon was so caring and concerned for my happiness.

But, ultimately, I wouldn't be happy if he was in danger.

"Then what do we do? Everyone freaked out about Nash in a costume. Abby, Dr. Meadows, the TV station. If they find out there really is a werewolf in town . . . who knows what they will do? I just know it won't be good."

Brandon stared off into the woods. "I've caused you enough trouble already," he said.

"Caused me trouble? This isn't about me—it's about you."

"I don't care about me. I'm more worried about what will happen to you if everyone finds out you're dating a werewolf. I can't do that to you." He leaned against a tree, as if we'd both been defeated. "There's only one thing to do for now."

"Yes?" I asked, hopeful he had a romantic solution. I imagined he'd suggest we run away together or meet again to figure out another plan.

Instead he appeared sullen again. "It's best we stay apart," he said firmly.

"What?" I asked, stunned. "But I don't want that."

"I want you to continue to hang out with your friends. I want you to continue to do what you've been doing. Until I find a cure."

"You find a cure? Alone? I'm not going to just forget about you and go back to a normal life like these past few months haven't even happened." I took his hand and drew myself to him. "I don't want us to be apart." I leaned my head on his chest. He was trying to resist, but he caved in and held me.

"Then promise me something." He took my chin and lifted it so I'd see him.

"What?" I asked. Everyone was asking me for promises I didn't want to make. They weren't the promises of love and romance that I was always looking for but promises of not seeing Brandon.

"That we'll only see each other in secret. Until I find a cure. This is the only way I know no harm will come to you."

I had to do what was best for him. In this case, Brandon was in much more danger of losing his life than I was of losing my friends by not sharing my secret with them.

"I want to tell them," I said, tears welling in my eyes. "I want us to be normal. I want us to be together."

"But I am not normal . . ." he began, softly tucking my hair behind my ears. "Not now, anyway. And when I am cured, it will be safe for you. But only when that happens."

"Nash will think he won," I said, tormented.

"This isn't about Nash. It is about you."

Brandon was asking me to wait. "If it's for my own good," I asked, "then why does it hurt so much?"

He continued to caress my hair, trying to comfort me. But to me, it wasn't about what *I'd* be going through. I could bear the thought of being teased, but I couldn't bear putting Brandon's safety at risk.

"No one will know," I said, finally resigned.

He took my hands and placed them to his lips.

"You'll have to find a cure before the next full moon," I

said, melting underneath his romantic spell. "I really want to tell the world I'm dating you. But for now you'll be my best-kept secret."

He leaned in and gave me a juicy kiss.

I continued to hug Brandon and noticed the suds had dripped down the side of his Jeep, erasing the word *WOLF-MAN*.

It pained me to no end to see the struggle that Brandon's condition presented to him. If only everyone in town could see how gorgeous and magnetic he was when he transformed, and that he should be admired, not feared. But change was scary in this town, and outsiders were even more so. A werewolf was a werewolf, and it would be hard to convince anyone that Brandon was a handsome and benevolent one—that he was more tormented by his own condition than anyone else should be.

But I knew that what I was hoping for was impossible. We had three weeks to find a cure for Brandon and make him one of the ordinary students of Legend's Run before another full moon appeared. But even then, Brandon Maddox was anything but ordinary.

TWO

seeking solutions

It was time to find a cure for Brandon. I was more focused on it than I'd ever been. If we could find a cure for him turning into a werewolf, then we'd be able to deal with the singular conflict of me dating a Westsider.

Ivy, Abby, and I were in the school library, and I was surfing the net for anything that could help solve Brandon's lycan condition while they were occupied with a pile of magazines. However, in my surfing, I wasn't finding anything that seemed reasonable and was becoming increasingly frustrated.

Annoyed, I was tapping my nails against the keys when Ivy placed her hand on mine.

"Stop!" she said. "What are you so worked up about?"

"Oh . . . nothing."

"Are you still thinking about werewolves?" Ivy asked,

looking up from her rag mag and peering at the screen. "We know that Brandon was the costumed stalker. And your report is done. What gives?"

"Uh . . ." I switched to the school's home page. "I don't know. It just stuck with me."

"Are you trying to cure the Wolfman?" Ivy teased. "You're always helping out the underprivileged."

"He's not underprivileged, Ivy."

"Well, he isn't one of us." She rolled her eyes and returned to her mag.

I know, I know, I thought. I didn't want to be reminded that my friends didn't approve of outsiders.

"I'm thinking of having a party this weekend," Abby said. "Ivy and Nash had one, so it's my turn. Then it will be yours, Celeste."

I couldn't imagine hosting a party at my house. Our house was modest, not the grand estates my friends called home. We had a few rooms, but they were filled with hand-knit blankets, outdated sofas, and decades-old carpeting instead of designer decor.

"Well, speaking of werewolves," I said. "Maybe we could invite Brandon?" I asked gingerly.

"There she goes again," Ivy protested. "You are always stuck on him. You feel bad for him because everyone's been calling him Wolfman?"

"Including you," I said. "And yes, I do."

"Well, I kind of do, too," Abby said.

"You do?" Ivy and I asked in unison. I was happy that I had someone on my side, but I could tell by Ivy's tone of "you do?" that she felt betrayed.

"He did find Pumpkin," Abby said. "I was distraught without her."

"Yes, that was a nice thing to do," Ivy said. "But you've seen how he eats. Those gloves. He's weird."

I took Abby's positive remark as an opportunity to continue to bring Brandon into the mix. "I think inviting him to your party would be a great way to pay him back," I said. "Someone vandalized his car, so I'm sure he's feeling awful. This could be an olive-branch opportunity if we included him."

"Uh . . . sure," Abby said. "What's one more?"

Ivy rolled her eyes. She didn't like Abby being more amiable than her.

"That would be great!" I said.

"Are you kidding?" Ivy said. "Just like that? Let him into your house?"

"He was at Nash's and seemed pretty normal," Abby said.

"You don't think people will talk?" Ivy asked. "All the popular students, and then him?"

"Let them," I said. "Maybe it will be fun to be the center of gossip for a change."

"Everyone thinks he was the werewolf," Ivy challenged.

"So, maybe he is," I said. "But it won't be a full moon for a few more weeks." I gave her a shot back.

"This will be cool," Abby said. "I did want to do something

for him—for finding Pumpkin, but I didn't know what. I feel good about this. Thanks for suggesting it, Celeste."

Ivy snarled under her breath. "Awesome, I do, too," she said. "Why don't we pick him up?" Ivy asked sarcastically. "Celeste and me. We can bring him to your house," she teased.

I seized this opportunity as well. "That's a great idea!" I said.

"But I was just—" Ivy tried.

"I knew you guys had soft spots in you," I said. "I'm so proud of you both."

"It'll be fun to have a werewolf at the party," Abby said. "People will be talking about it for ages."

I was happily daydreaming in third bell, imagining Brandon at Abby's party. I envisioned Abby and me giving him a tour of her house, he and I exchanging glances from across the room and stealing a kiss in her garage when she needed extra drinks.

After fourth bell, I closely followed Abby and Ivy as they approached Brandon at his locker with their mission.

"I'm going to have a party this weekend," Abby said. "And you should come."

Brandon appeared surprised by their friendly conversation and invite.

"Excuse me?" he asked skeptically.

"I'm having a party Friday and would like to invite you,"

Abby said, adjusting her ponytail.

I stepped out from behind them. Brandon noticed me, and his skeptical expression brightened. We locked eyes, and for a moment, I was lost in his gaze.

Abby must have noticed because she nudged me. I blushed and twisted my beaded necklace.

"I'd like to repay you for finding my dog," Abby said to Brandon.

Abby was the tallest of us girls, but even she didn't stand as tall as Brandon. He smiled down warmly at my friend, and I wasn't sure she wasn't going to blush as well. "You don't have to repay me," he said sincerely.

"No," she said. "I insist you come."

"Celeste and Ivy will pick you up," Abby instructed. "Be ready at nine."

Brandon was taken aback. "You are going to pick me up?" he asked Ivy.

"Yes," Abby answered for her. "They'll be your escorts."

"Well, this is really cool," he said with a radiant smile.

"You'll want to come," Ivy said in her bossy voice. "What else do you have to do?"

I gave him a quick wink, and we moved to our lockers.

"Did you see the way he was looking at you?" Ivy said to me. "Like a wolf on fresh meat. He's always staring at you. I think he likes you."

"Good thing you are going out with Nash," Abby said. "Otherwise, you could be dating him."

"Ooh!" Ivy cringed.

My friends cracked up. It was comments like that that made it hard for me to burst out the news that I was in love with Brandon.

That afternoon, I was hanging out at Brandon's guesthouse. The air was still too chilly to spend any time outside without his werewolf form to keep me warm.

We were sitting on top of his bed watching TV, our legs intertwined, sharing a bowl of popcorn.

"That was nice of Abby to invite me to her party," he said. "But if you hadn't been with them, I'd think they were up to something sneaky."

"No, Abby really wants you to come."

"Abby? Or you?" He was skeptical.

"Well, both, silly."

"I thought you might be behind this . . ."

"No, she really wants you to come. They also think they are inviting a werewolf to the party," I confessed softly.

"Uh . . . they are."

"Isn't that ironic?" I asked. We both laughed. His gorgeous smile radiated like before.

"Yes. Fortunately the full moon is still a few weeks away. I've been trying to find a solution. But I haven't found anything."

Deep down I couldn't help but wait impatiently for the full moon to appear. As a werewolf, Brandon had a magnetic and spellbinding quality that I couldn't bear to be without.

"At this point, I might do anything," he said. "I don't want to be a werewolf and I don't want us to be apart." He gazed at me longingly. "Maybe I should meet Dr. Meadows."

Dr. Meadows was the psychic who originally predicted that I'd be in a snowfall surrounded by wolves and warned me against kissing a werewolf. I had returned to her for help for Brandon, but ultimately she was more interested in getting fame and attention for herself than finding a cure for him.

"We can't go back to Dr. Meadows," I said. "We can't trust her."

"Then what do we do?" Brandon was frustrated. He stood up and paced in his room.

"I think we should go back to Charlie and see if he has any ideas," I said.

I'd discovered my favorite resident at Pine Tree Village Retirement Community, Mr. Charlie Worthington, was Brandon's great-grandfather. The elderly man was keen on his Legend's Run werewolf folklore and liked to talk about how the original creature of the moonlight was his great-grandfather.

Brandon seemed pleased with my idea as his dark mood lifted. We grabbed our coats, and he locked his guesthouse door. He politely opened the passenger door of his Jeep and helped me inside, then drove us to Pine Tree Village.

Mr. Worthington was sitting on the couch in the foyer

with an inviting grin, greeting all guests.

"What a nice surprise," he said, rising. "It's not even the weekend."

"I'm not here to volunteer," I said. "We want to know more about the Legend's Run werewolf."

"Sit down, please." He was excited to have an eager audience. "Hold my calls," he said to the receptionist, who cracked a smile.

"Do you remember if he was ever cured?" I asked him.

Mr. Worthington took a moment to recollect. "No, I'm sorry to say he never was."

Brandon sighed.

I, too, was disappointed. I was hoping for some magic answers that the Legend's Run werewolf had discovered that helped him become human again.

"He lived the rest of his life as a werewolf," Mr. Worthington said, "if you believe it in the first place."

"We believe it," I said. But I was bummed thinking that Brandon, too, would have to spend his entire life running from the full moon.

"I think you're among the few who do," Mr. Worthington went on. "So why, may I ask, are you two so convinced that my great-grandfather, Brandon's ancestor, was a werewolf?"

Because Brandon is one, I wanted to say. But I was afraid that Mr. Worthington would have a heart attack right in front of us.

"I just think it's possible," I said. "And you are so convincing."

"Your mother did have a wild streak in her," he said to Brandon. "But you seem to have turned out fine."

"I'm not so sure," Brandon said.

"Why not? You have a nice girlfriend. Don't tell me you are a wild child, too."

"I wouldn't say that normally," Brandon said. "But some things have changed . . ."

"Ah, your teen years, that's all," Mr. Worthington reassured. "I shouldn't have told you that story. Now you'll think you are a werewolf, too!" Mr. Worthington laughed.

When we didn't join in his laughter, Mr. Worthington grew concerned.

"Did I offend you?" he said.

"Of course not," we both replied.

"You don't seem to be the serious type," he went on. "I thought I could poke a bit of fun."

"But we are still interested in your stories," Brandon interjected. "Is there any more you can tell us about the legend? About my family?"

"Ah . . . yes." Mr. Worthington appeared delighted that we—or rather that anyone—was interested in his stories. Many of the seniors at the retirement home longed to talk about their past, but when no one came to visit them, the stories were left to be heard by busy staffers, nurses, or doctors.

"He lived in isolation. Every time there was a full moon,

he roamed the woods alone, tormented by his condition—afraid he'd attack and afraid of being hunted down. Naturally the townsfolk were always trying to find 'the wild creature cursed by the moonlight.' There were those who said their livestock were mauled by him, and even a story in which a man claimed to be attacked by him. But without photos or other proof, they were just thought to be only stories."

"Did anyone try to help your great-grandfather?" Brandon asked.

"Yes. The local Native American chieftain and several gypsies. Potions, salves, and spells. But nothing kept the full moonlight from changing him. Eventually he fled into the woods and never returned."

I was saddened by his fate. Brandon hung his head low.

"I've often thought that is why your mother was so restless," Mr. Worthington continued. "I can't understand her behavior—not being responsible. Maybe it is just me trying to justify her behavior. But it is reprehensible."

Brandon pushed his hair back off his face.

"But I see you have done fine, Brandon," Mr. Worthington said. "Your father takes great care of you."

"Yes. And now my grandparents do as well."

"And you have this beautiful young lady here. You seem to have it all."

"Yes, except one thing," Brandon said.

"What is that?" Mr. Worthington wondered aloud.

"The answer to the mystery of your story." Brandon leaned in toward his elderly relative. "What could cure the werewolf?"

"Ah . . . yes," Mr. Worthington said. "That is what you came to find out? I think that is left up to science. Or the mystics. Or the imagination."

"Mystics?" I asked. I wasn't sure about going back to Dr. Meadows. But maybe we were supposed to heed Mr. Worthington's advice.

"Science," Brandon said as if that was the answer he'd been waiting for. "That's just what I had in mind."

"I guess we have to go to Dr. Meadows," I said to Brandon when we got back into his Jeep.

"Charlie gave us the answer," Brandon said. "My father."

"But your dad isn't a mystic."

"I know. He's a scientist."

"But isn't he in Europe?" I asked. Then I paused. "Does that mean you'll have to go there?"

"I don't know. I just know I have to tell him," Brandon said. "But he's going to freak out."

"He'll want to come and get you, won't he?" I was worried that if his father took him back with him to Europe, I might never see Brandon again.

"Everything happened so fast," Brandon said. "The thought of telling my dad—I was hoping to get this solved by myself. But I see now that I can't."

Of course I wanted Brandon to tell his father—we needed him to tell him. But I didn't want his father to take him away from Legend's Run and back to Miller's Glen or as far away as Europe.

"He's a busy man—and an ocean away. He's going to totally flip out," Brandon said when he pulled into his drive.

We both were lost in thought as he drove down his tree-lined driveway and parked by his guesthouse.

"How do you call your father and say, 'Hey, Dad, I think I'm a werewolf'?" Brandon appeared overwhelmed by the task at hand and leaned back in his seat.

"Maybe you should invite him here," I said. "Tell him you need him to come home—and plan it just before the full moon appears. Then you won't need to tell him. Instead, he'll see it."

Brandon was considering my suggestion, but he still appeared troubled. "I hate to be a burden to him. His job is important. Many people rely on him. It's not like he has a job where he can just come home for lunch. He's in Europe."

"But you're his son. No job is more important than that. He'll understand."

"I know . . . but he'll think I'm crazy."

If Brandon's father thought he was crazy, it wouldn't be good for either of us.

"Do you think he will make you leave Legend's Run?" I asked, concerned.

"I don't know. I don't know what he'll do. But I'm not

going anywhere." Then he placed his hand on mine. "Not without you."

I didn't want Brandon to leave, but I didn't want to be so selfish that I stood in the way of his being cured.

I unbuckled my seat belt and scooted close to him. "You have to call him. I know it will be awkward. But I know you can do it. I'll stay with you if you'd like."

"I think this is something I have to do alone."

I put my free hand on his knee. His green cargo pants were thick, but I could still feel his toned leg, strong from skating and working on his grandparents' property.

I wanted him to know I was there for him. Didn't Brandon do everything on his own already? Eat lunch, study, live life as a werewolf. It broke my heart to see him have to face another moment alone.

"Are you sure?" I asked.

"Yes. I'll call you as soon as I talk to him. If I hurry, I might be able to catch him before he goes to bed."

This meant I'd have to go home; I didn't want to leave Brandon's side. I wanted to stay and help him.

He got out of the Jeep, preoccupied. The impending phone call was causing him major stress. He barely made eye contact.

"It will be okay," I reassured him as I opened my car door.

"Always the cheerleader," he said. "Hey, why aren't you one? You'd look cute in those short, pleated skirts."

"I tried out and didn't make it," I said. "Freshman year. I

guess I'm not coordinated enough. So I cheer from the stands instead."

Brandon's blue eyes and red-hot lips blazed. He leaned into me and kissed me, long. I wasn't about to let go. But then he broke away.

"I'll call you," he said, caressing my cheek with the back of his hand. He leaned in and gave me a hug and another kiss. "I couldn't do this without you," he said.

But Brandon wouldn't have been in this situation without me, either. I was torn.

I got into my car and drove away, my heart aching for him and imagining him making the hardest call of his life.

I paced inside my home and waited impatiently for Brandon's call.

He will be here in time for the full moon.

It was after midnight when I finally got the text. I was unable to sleep, read, or write and was trying to ease my mind by watching a romantic comedy. When I read his text, a wave of relief flowed through me. Brandon's father was coming to his rescue, like Brandon had come to mine when I'd been lost in the wintry woods and stumbled upon the pack of wolves. His father was a genius scientist and surely would be able to figure out what Brandon needed to do. It was good that Brandon was finally going to trust someone else with the secret of his lycan condition.

But what if Brandon was cured and this full moon would

be his last? Was that something I really wanted? Of course, I knew it was, but there was a piece of me that would be haunted by not being with the werewolf that I'd loved.

I'd miss our moments together in the snowy woods, surrounded by playful and gentle wolves, his super-strength, powerful and sultry kisses, and über-hot body. I'd have to say good-bye to his unearthly magnetism that I couldn't get out of my skin; his sensual woodsy smell that remained on my clothes and hair; his divine touch that kept me warm in the coldest of temperatures. I was happy for him but sort of sad for me. These experiences would be only cherished memories.

But the important thing was Brandon would be normal, and he and I could officially date. Maybe my friends could finally accept him into our pack.

THREE

party with a werewolf

I can't believe we are actually doing this," Ivy said when I got into her mom's Lexus SUV and we drove off to pick up Brandon and take him to Abby's party. I was excited to be seeing Brandon in public even though we still weren't open about our relationship. And I thought it would be good for both of us to have a little fun since we had about two weeks until his father was coming in from Europe.

"Doesn't it make you feel good, doing something nice for someone else?"

"Kind of. But I don't want to get in the habit of this," she said with a smile.

"We'll be the talk of the party."

"Well, it will be awesome to have the Legend's Run were-wolf at the party." She didn't know that she was speaking the truth. "Maybe he'll even wear the costume," she said hopefully.

"It wasn't even his," I said defensively.

"How can you be so sure?" she asked.

I wanted to tell her it was Nash who had hidden inside the costume, but if it got back to him that I'd told her, he would surely tell her he'd seen me in the woods with Brandon.

"I just know . . ." I said.

"Always sticking up for people," Ivy said. "That's why you rock."

Ivy began driving us through the west side of Legend's Run. "What if a killer jumps out of the woods?" she asked suddenly.

She wasn't used to being in desolate areas, and I was only somewhat used to it because I'd been visiting Brandon the last few months. But Ivy was freaked out by the lack of traffic and population.

"Do you think we'll make it out of here alive?"

"Yes," I reassured her.

"What if we get a flat tire? And our cell phones don't work? No one will know we're in trouble and some psycho—"

"Calm down," I said.

"You have to admit, it's totally creepy back here. Like some horror flick. Why didn't we bring Jake with us?"

I could see why she thought it was frightening, with shadows casting spooky images off of the trees and road. It could make one's imagination race. But I enjoyed the peace the country brought and felt calmed by the quiet.

"It's not that much farther," I said. I was anxious to get to his house, too, but for different reasons.

"Why would anyone want to live back here?" she asked. "There aren't any lights. And there's nothing to do."

"Some people like wide-open spaces and nature," I said. "There is so much to do. Hike, canoe, camp. You might even like it."

"There isn't a mall," she said with a laugh. "Enough said."

Finally we turned onto Brandon's street, and I pointed to the private drive sign a few yards away.

She pulled into his driveway and drove down the long, tree-lined road. "Where is this leading us to?" Ivy asked. "I know it's not a country club."

"Just keep going," I said.

It didn't take long before his grandparents' house was in view.

"It's so cute and tiny," she said when we got close.

Ivy parked the car in front of the main house, and the Lexus's lights shone on the guesthouse.

"Who lives back there?" she said. "Some madman?"

I wasn't going to tell her that was Brandon's guesthouse, nor was I going to admit to her how I knew it.

Brandon's grandparents' husky began barking like mad in the window.

"Do we have to go in?" she asked. "I'm afraid to get out of the car."

Just then someone was standing by Ivy's window.

She screamed a bloodcurdling scream, causing me to scream, too.

"What's wrong?" I said, my heart almost busting out of my chest. Then I caught my breath and noticed a familiar smile. "It's just Brandon."

She lowered her window. "You almost scared me to death!" she said.

Even in the darkness, Brandon was gorgeous. His eyes matched the color of his bright blue shirt. It was hard for me not to stare and even harder for me not to kiss him.

"I appreciate you picking me up," Brandon said, hopping into the backseat. "This is very cool of you."

"Well, it is the least we can do," Ivy said, "after you found Abby's dog and all."

"Man, I'll be the luckiest guy there," he said. "Showing up with the two most beautiful girls in school."

Ivy's face flushed. She was flattered by his attention and politeness. Jake and Dylan spent most of their time goofing off in front of their girlfriends.

"This part of town is really interesting," Ivy said, suddenly in flirt mode. "I've always thought it was charming."

What? I thought. The compliments had gone to her head.

"It might be easier if you turn around," he said. "Saves you backing up."

"Ah," she said. "Good idea."

She drove forward and turned around in front of

Brandon's guesthouse. The lights illuminated part of the huge backyard.

"This is all yours?" she asked.

"My grandparents'," he replied.

The lot was bigger than hers, and she was impressed.

Then we spotted the Jeep, which was parked off to the side.

"That was a shame someone vandalized your Jeep," she said, now concerned. "But it looks like you got it all off."

"Yes," he said. "I did have some help."

I nervously tucked my hair behind my ear.

"So . . . how do you like it here in Legend's Run?" I asked as Ivy finished making her U-turn and began down the drive.

"It's been okay."

"You don't seem to have a lot of friends," Ivy said.

"I have the one I need," he said. Now my face flushed.

"That skater chick, Hayley?" she asked. "She's your girlfriend?"

"No, she's not," he said.

"Do you have a girlfriend?" she asked, looking in the rearview mirror.

"I'd like to think so."

"Then who is she?" Ivy pried. "Do we know her?"

"Yes, I think you do."

"You must tell!" Ivy said, excited to get the goods on any gossip she could, no matter what side of town it was coming from.

"Do you miss Miller's Glen?" I asked, changing the subject.

Ivy snarled, and I could tell she was let down by not getting the latest scoop.

"I'm starting to like it here," he said.

"Well, if you haven't noticed, this town is really cliquey," Ivy said as if she wasn't part of making that happen. "I don't know why, but that's the way it's always been. Too bad, really."

We parked outside Abby's house. There was already a line of cars, including Nash's Beemer. I wasn't sure how he'd respond to Brandon being at the party, but with Ivy bringing him, I figured he wouldn't make a scene.

Abby opened the door, and we were immediately greeted by Pumpkin. She raced up to Brandon, who petted her like she was his own.

Abby gave Ivy and me a quick hug.

"Hi, Brandon," she said. "Come on in."

Abby struggled, trying to pull Pumpkin by her collar so she wouldn't continue to jump on Brandon.

"It looks like she missed you," Abby said.

It took a little bit of time for Pumpkin to calm down. Abby was trying to wrangle her in when Brandon locked gazes with the dog.

Pumpkin relaxed by his side. Then Brandon petted her again.

"You have a way with dogs," Abby said.

We hovered in the two-story, open foyer. Abby's father's office was on one side and a grand dining room was on the other. Their furniture was too expensive to sit on, and the house looked like a model home.

Jake and Dylan and a few others who were lingering in the foyer were obviously shocked to see Brandon in our company.

"What's he doing here?" Jake mumbled to Ivy. "And why did you and Celeste pick him up?"

"Abby wanted to invite him to pay him back for finding Pumpkin," she said.

Dylan wasn't pleased, either. He took Abby by the arm and whispered something I couldn't hear.

"It's okay," she said, brushing him off. "It's just a party."

"Come on in, guys," she said. "Do you want a drink, Brandon?"

Abby was being a great hostess. We followed her through the kitchen.

"Hey, Wolfie," Jake said as we passed by. Ivy pinched his elbow.

"Knock it off," she said sternly.

I was proud to see my friends sticking up for Brandon.

Abby led the way into the main room, with Pumpkin at Brandon's heels. A bunch of students were already drinking, talking, and having a good time. All eyes were on us as the partygoers were surprised to see an outsider like Brandon at Abby's party.

Abby handed us sodas and we stood around awkwardly. It didn't take long for Ivy to hang with Jake while Abby attended to her party.

Brandon and I were left to hang out with each other. Normally I would have been excited, but since he wasn't my established boyfriend, I couldn't be cozy with him like my friends and the rest of the couples were being.

"Where's Nash?" Ivy asked, her arms draped on Jake as they hung out on the couch.

"I think he's out back," he replied.

I'd been hoping Nash would have been there when we first arrived with Ivy. Then he would have seen the three of us girls together with Brandon, and it would have been less jarring. The way it was now, it looked like I'd brought Brandon. And though I didn't mind that, I didn't want to shove it in Nash's face, since it really wasn't why Brandon was here.

Brandon and I hung together. I wanted so badly to lean against him, hold his hand, snuggle up to him. He was so close to me, I could smell the fabric softener on his clothes and the cologne on his skin. It made for a heavenly mix; the scent was driving me crazy.

A cool burst of air flowed through the house as Nash came in from outside. He had a huge grin on his face until he saw me standing with Brandon. Then his smile turned to a spiteful frown.

He smelled like cigarette smoke. Nash didn't approve of smoking, so I was curious whose company he'd been in.

"Well, if it isn't the Wolfman," Nash said.

The group of partygoers looked to see Brandon's reaction.

"Nash—" Abby said suddenly, coming in from the kitchen. "I thought we lost you."

"I was just getting some air and I come back to find—"

"I invited Brandon to the party," she said.

"You did?"

"Yes, he saved Pumpkin so I wanted to invite him." Abby spoke low but forcefully.

Pumpkin was still at Brandon's side.

"By the looks of it you'd think Pumpkin was his dog," Dylan said. We watched as Brandon petted Pumpkin.

"So you two are still seeing each other?" Nash whispered to me. I could hear the jealousy in his voice. I didn't want to upset him, but it wasn't like Nash had been so in love with me when we were dating. He acted a lot different now that we weren't. Nash put his arm around me. I quickly wiggled out. "Do Ivy and Abby know about him and you?" he whispered again. "And what I saw?"

"Shh!" I said softly. "No one knows."

Abby pulled Pumpkin away from Brandon as the dog continued to want to be in his company. She opened the back door to let Pumpkin out and Heidi Rosen and a few other girls came in from outside. They all smelled like smoke. It was apparent Nash hadn't missed me that much.

The way Heidi and the girls looked at us told me that our plan may have backfired. Bringing Brandon didn't ensure him new popularity. It only ensured him being more ostracized than before.

We weren't being affectionate, but since no one was including Brandon in their conversation and I wanted to spend time with him, I stayed near him. But it was impossible to get any alone time with Brandon now that Nash was inside. Nash followed us around, surveyed every move Brandon and I made, and tried to stand between us whenever possible. Ivy and Abby were both absorbed in their own missions—Ivy enjoying Jake, and Abby enjoying being a hostess, so I couldn't hang out with them and not be tempted to show my affection for Brandon.

"So are you taking Brandon home, too?" Jake asked Ivy. "I don't like you bringing other guys to parties. It looks bad. But I definitely don't want you taking other guys home from parties."

"We'll drive him home," Nash said.

"Yes," Dylan confirmed. "We can have a chat with our new friend."

My mind raced, and the images were horrible. And though our boyfriends weren't violent, nothing good was to come of them taking him home.

"No—I will make sure he gets home," I said.

"But you don't have a car," Abby noted.

"It's only right, since we brought him," I said.

"Now we are fighting over him," Ivy gushed.

"I can make my own decisions," Brandon said.

"I don't think it's a good idea for you to be driven home by our girlfriends," said Nash.

"Your girlfriends?" Brandon pressed. "Do you mean Celeste?"

Nash knew exactly what Brandon meant.

"Guys, let's cool it," I said.

"I can call a cab," Brandon offered. "In fact, I'll call one now." He reached in his pocket and pulled out his phone.

"A cab?" Nash said. "I don't think they drive to the Westside. They might get shot."

"That's it," I said. "I'll take you home."

Nash snarled.

"You don't even have a car." Ivy repeated Abby's remark.

"We can walk to my house from here. Then I can drive Brandon back. He's our guest, and I'm not going to let him be treated like this."

"Let's calm down," Abby said. "This is a party, guys."

"I think it's getting ugly," I said. "We aren't having a good time, Abby. I'm sorry, but some of your guests don't know how to behave."

"Dylan, do something," Abby pressed.

Her boyfriend raised his hand as if to stop us. "Don't let the door hit you on the way out," he teased. Abby tossed a sofa pillow at him.

Ivy got up. "I don't want to drive back to the Westside

now," she said to me. "We just got here. I'll try to cool the guys down."

"Don't worry," I said. "You stay. I'll take him back."

"But you'll be all alone with him," she told me.

"I'll be okay. There's nothing at all to worry about. You saw—he's very polite."

"Now I feel really bad. He was really polite and we brought him to a party where the guys were awful. This was supposed to be fun, not like school."

"I know," Abby whined. "I wanted to be a good hostess."

"Don't worry," I reassured her, giving her a hug. "You were."

"I'm sorry, Brandon," Abby apologized. "I really wish you'd both stay."

"That's okay," Brandon said. "I appreciate the invite."

"At least Pumpkin was nice to him," I said, shrugging my shoulders.

"I don't want you to go so soon." Ivy pouted.

I wasn't coming out and proclaiming my love for Brandon to them, but I hoped my actions said something. Even if I didn't have such strong romantic feelings for him, I'd still have stuck up for him. I didn't like to see my friends treating someone so badly. Nash and the guys were acting up, and it was inappropriate behavior.

Nash was fuming. I was leaving the party with another guy—a Westsider. And to make it worse, there wasn't anything he could do about it.

"Please call me when you get there," Ivy directed. "Promise?"

"Of course," I said as I headed to the front door.

Ivy was always motherly to me, from that first day I'd met her on the bus. She liked to take care of me. It was one of her most endearing qualities.

"Sorry about that," I said when I caught up to Brandon. He was waiting at the lamppost by the walk in the front yard.

"Nash is just fighting for you. I can't blame him."

"You are too kind," I said. I pulled the collar of my coat up to cover my blushing cheeks.

"People are really going to talk now," he said, "with you taking me home."

"Let them. I think I've been waiting for it. But I'm more concerned about the repercussions for you."

"Well, if Nash does tell them what he saw . . ." he lamented.

"Then I'll tell them he's joking."

We started walking in the direction of my house.

"Well, anyway," he began, "I think I'm getting used to it."

"Are you?" I asked. It hurt me deep inside to know that Brandon was becoming accustomed to the negative treatment by my friends, their boyfriends, and other students at school. "How can you?"

"I just focus on you."

"That's so sweet." I linked my arm with his and squeezed

him. "But it must be hard. You don't deserve to be treated the way you are. Our school is so cliquey."

"I think they all are," he said.

"Was it like that in Miller's Glen?"

He nodded.

"So you were teased there, too?"

Instead of answering, Brandon wrapped his arm around my shoulder. I felt warm in his embrace. However, when he was a werewolf, he really emanated heat.

"So now we have the rest of the night together," he said. "Just us."

"Yes, just us."

"What would you like to do?" he asked as we walked out of Abby's community and down the sidewalk toward my subdivision. "See a movie?"

There was so much I wanted to do with Brandon. See a movie, shop at the mall, watch a game. All the things I was used to doing I wanted to experience with him.

We continued to stroll, huddling closely together, when we turned the corner to my community.

"Would you like to come inside?" I asked. I'd rarely invited Nash inside my house. Since his house was so large and mine more modest, I always felt like he might think he was dating down. Even though Brandon's grandparents had acres of land and vast woods surrounding his home, he didn't seem to be the type to be bothered by such things. And even if Nash didn't come out and say anything, I felt self-conscious. But with Brandon, I felt like material status didn't matter. I could hear Champ inside barking as we walked up the sidewalk.

"Sure. That sounds awesome."

My parents had gone out for the night to dinner and a movie, so they wouldn't be home for a while. I thought it was a good opportunity to be alone with Brandon, without the usual parental annoyances.

Brandon followed me inside and was greeted enthusiastically by Champ, who wagged his tail and panted in excitement. As I began to close the door behind us, I noticed a car driving down the street. It was Nash's BMW. I quickly shut the door and heard him drive away.

I removed my coat and scarf and took Brandon's as well. I wanted to be the perfect hostess. I hung his coat in the hall closet instead of leaving it on the banister, as I tended to do with mine.

Brandon seemed eager to explore the house and poked his head around our entryway. Champ followed him as if he were his owner.

"You want the official tour?" I asked.

"Sure."

"I think it will take half a minute," I said with a nervous chuckle.

"No—your house is really cool."

"Well, it's not like Abby's. Or Nash's."

"Why should it be?"

Brandon was right. A burst of energy raced through me

with his warm compliment.

"Here's our dining room," I said, leading him around. I couldn't help but have an extra bounce in my step. Champ was still glued to Brandon. I had to drag him outside to give Brandon room to breathe. "This is our kitchen and family room. And the bedrooms are upstairs."

As we both stood in my kitchen, I was nervous. Even though I'd been over to Brandon's home many times, I felt awkward. After all, he had his own guesthouse, a hilltop that went on for days, and his own skating rink.

I obsessively tucked my hair behind my ear and kept on wriggling in my stance.

"As you can see, it's not a castle like Nash's and Abby's."

"I think this house is great. It has character, like you."

His smile melted me, and he took my hands. "I've been waiting to do this all night."

I'd been waiting, too, since I first saw him get into Ivy's SUV. He drew me into him and kissed me long and with such passion I had to lean against the island so as not to faint.

Here I was standing in my kitchen kissing Brandon Maddox. It was so far from anything that I'd ever imagined happening.

"We can hang out here," I said. I switched on the TV. "Maybe there's a movie on. What would you like to watch?"

"Aren't you going to show me your room?" he asked.

"It's a total mess. I wasn't expecting you to come over."

"I know. I just thought it would be nice to see where you

hang out. Then we can come back and watch TV."

I led him up the stairs, where a few of our family pictures lined the wall. I blushed as we passed one of me as a baby. "I hate that one."

"No—it's cute."

"It's so dumb. I barely had any hair."

"Well, you could be like me—and a few nights a month have too much."

We both laughed.

It was weird. I felt so buzzed having Brandon in my house alone with me. And to think that he was also a werewolf—an attractive one—made me feel even more freaked out.

"Wow—" he said. "This is cool."

My room was painted light blue with dark blue curtains. We hadn't redone my room in years, and now I wasn't sure if I wished I had. I had a dusty porcelain horse collection, stacks of worn books on shelves, and my laptop computer on my hand-me-down desk.

I noticed a pink bra resting on my hamper. I raced over to it, hoping he wouldn't notice it before I retrieved it. I felt embarrassed as I lifted the lid and quickly threw it inside.

"So, do you want to go back downstairs now?" I asked.

"No, this is awesome." He wandered around my room, examining my pictures and figurines.

His jersey was still on my nightstand. I had shown it to him to prove he had taken it off the first time he'd turned but hadn't given it back. Since he hadn't asked for it to be returned, I kept it on my nightstand. I'd never admit it to him, but sometimes I even held it when I slept.

"You still have my shirt," he said.

"I was hoping you wouldn't see that."

He reached out to me and took my hands, then pulled me into him. I felt like he was going to kiss me—right here in my room. Here, where I'd dreamed about him so many nights and written his name a dozen times in every one of my notebooks.

Brandon wasn't a star running back, but he might as well have been. He was all muscle; I felt small and dainty in his presence.

He cupped my face in his warm hands and drew me in and kissed me.

"Now are you ready to go downstairs?" he asked.

"Uh . . . not yet." I leaned in for another kiss when I heard the sound of the garage door opening.

"My parents are here!" I said. "They weren't supposed to be back this soon!"

He laughed at how flustered I'd become. "I guess your dad might get upset if he came home and found me in your bedroom."

"Good thing it's not a full moon—or we'd really be in trouble," I said.

My older sister, Juliette, had guys in her room all the time when she lived at home. But I didn't have the reputation my sister had and was hoping to avoid one.

Brandon and I raced downstairs. The TV was switched on to QVC—not the sort of show two seventeen-year-olds were usually engrossed in on a Friday night. It screamed, *We were making out!*

I quickly turned it to a movie channel when the mud-room door opened.

"What are you doing home?" my mom asked when she entered the family room. Then she noticed Brandon sitting next to me. "Oh, hi," she said. "I didn't know you had company."

Brandon rose and extended his hand to my parents.

"This is Brandon," I said. "Brandon, these are my parents."

My dad gave Brandon a firm handshake. He seemed surprised to see a boy in our house.

"I thought you were at Abby's party," my mom said.

"We were, but Brandon needed a ride home so we stopped off here to get my car. And we decided to watch TV for a little bit."

"The movie we wanted to see was sold out," my dad said, "so we're going to have to wait to see it tomorrow."

"That's nice," I said, not knowing what to say.

"Well, don't let us keep you," my mom said.

My dad continued to hover.

"Uh . . . that's okay. I was just about to take Brandon home," I said.

"No—you two can watch TV," my mom offered.

"It's getting late," I said as we headed for our coats.

I didn't feel like letting my parents embarrass me with

their get-to-know-you banter, so I whisked Brandon out the front door.

When we got into the car, I switched on the radio. As I was flipping stations, "Fly Me to the Moon" was playing on an oldies hits station.

"That's our song!" I said.

Brandon and I sang along with Frank Sinatra, trying to remember all the words and the correct pitches and cracking up at ourselves. When the song was over, my gut was in pain from all the laughing.

I had just parked in front of his guesthouse when Ivy called.

"Where are you?" she asked. I could hear the sounds of partygoers in the background.

"I'm dropping Brandon off."

"Now? But you left ages ago. I was hoping you'd come back to the party."

"It took a little longer than I thought," I said, holding the phone away from Brandon.

"I was worried about you. You didn't call me."

"I'm fine."

"I'm sorry I didn't go with you. I guess I should have, but I wanted—"

"Don't worry about it, really," I said. I was thankful my friend had remained at the party. If not, I wouldn't have had time with Brandon at my house or now alone in my car.

"What was it like driving him by yourself? Did he make a

move?" she teased. I was dying to say we'd kissed only a short time ago. I signaled to Brandon, who was doing his best to be patient while I talked.

"Stop," I said. "Let me call you back when I get home. I don't want to drive and talk."

I hung up and turned toward Brandon. It was dark, but the moonlight shone brightly on his gorgeous features.

"I'm really sorry about the party," I said to Brandon. "It didn't go as planned."

"I don't mind," he said. "I got to be with you. See your room. Meet your parents. And get a kiss."

I blushed and we got out of the car. As we stood outside his guesthouse, he put his hands in his pockets and looked down at me.

"That was really nice of you to stick up for me in front of your friends," he said. "You are always doing that."

"I feel bad because I haven't told Ivy and Abby about us yet. You know I want to."

"But we agree why you shouldn't. It's not because I'm from the Westside. It because I'm a—"

"Well, hopefully we can have that fixed soon. It won't be long until your father comes here."

"Yes, and then we can finally be together."

"In the hallways," I said.

". . . and at lunch," he added.

". . . and everywhere," I confirmed.

We lingered for a moment, lost in romantic thought, and

then he pulled me in and kissed me.

"What are you doing tomorrow?" he asked.

"I was going to go to the game with Ivy and Abby. But I'd rather be with you."

"Maybe you should spend some time with them," he said, wrapping me in his arms. "Since you left tonight—they might be mad?"

"But I'd really rather be with you." I felt so warm and cozy in his embrace.

He leaned in and kissed me again. Heat rose throughout my body; I didn't want to be anywhere but on the other side of his lips. Then his dog began to bark, and a light came on in the main house's bedroom window and our moment was broken.

"Call me when you get home," he said, walking me to my car. "I want to make sure you're all right."

I had two guardians—Ivy and Brandon. Two polar opposites, but both my best friends.

The following day, I awoke early. I had spring fever. I was so ecstatic about being with Brandon that I couldn't contain myself. Not through sleep, studying, or talking on the phone. Midday, I met Ivy and Abby at Hotspots for coffee. I chose a tall decaf latte because I was already hyped up on Brandon.

"So what happened when you took him home?" Abby asked eagerly.

"Nothing really." But the memory of kissing Brandon

brought a huge smile to my face.

"Did he make any moves on you?" Abby asked.

"He said he had a girlfriend," Ivy said.

"He did?" Abby asked.

"Yes." Ivy was proud to have info that Abby wasn't privy to yet. "And he also said we know her. I still think it's that skater chick."

"Really?" Abby said. "He doesn't hang out with anyone at school."

"But she sits at his table," Ivy said.

"Not next to him," Abby challenged.

"Whoever she is," Ivy said, "I wouldn't want to be her."

My smile drooped. My best friend's comment stung. My stomach felt hollow, and pouring a latte into it wasn't going to make it feel better.

"Why not?" I said defensively. "There's nothing wrong with him. He was nice to you."

"Isn't she sweet, still taking pity on the needy?" Ivy asked.

"Why would you feel bad for his girlfriend?" I challenged her. "Everyone deserves love."

"You would think so," Ivy said with a grin.

"They do," I proclaimed. "And it's not right to keep judging people just because they live on the opposite side of town." I would have told my friend right there and then that I was the one who was in love with Brandon Maddox and it was me who he was referring to as the girlfriend that she knew. But as I gazed into her blue eyes, I recalled the intense gray of Brandon's werewolf eyes, and I knew that this wasn't about me being self-righteous but about him being safe.

"Relax," Ivy said. "I didn't mean to start an argument. I just feel bad because that girl obviously doesn't think enough of him to sit by him at lunch. That's all. I would think you'd agree with that."

I did agree. Brandon's girlfriend should sit with him, but since I was the one dating him and we had so many obstacles in our way, we didn't spend our lunch bell together. But again, I couldn't tell them all that.

"When you drove him home," Abby began, "didn't you ask him who she was?"

"Uh . . . no."

"You need to be nosier!" Ivy scolded. "Abby and I will find out."

"Maybe it's not our business," I said. "If he wanted us and the whole school to know, he'd be sitting with her, too."

"We'll get to the bottom of it," Ivy said. "No one is going to have a secret in this school without us knowing about it!" My friends giggled wildly.

"What happened at the party?" I asked, changing the subject. "What did I miss?"

"Nothing major," Abby said. "Jake lost his keys. Heidi Rosen spilled her drink on her skintight dress. Dylan broke my mom's Las Vegas snow globe. The usual party stuff."

"Have you talked to Nash since you left?" Ivy asked.

"No . . . not yet," I answered.

"He was really fuming," Ivy said. "He tried to hide it, but I could tell. He even left, saying he was going out to get some more drinks, but I sensed it was really to follow you."

"I think I saw him," I confessed.

"Yes, that was smart of you to take Brandon home," Ivy said. "It made Nash even crazier about you."

"But that's not why I did it."

"Well, either way, it worked," she told me.

"I hope you don't mind I didn't drive him back," Ivy said. "I wanted to stay at the party."

"No worries," I said.

"But I was hoping you'd come back," Ivy said.

"Yes, me too," Abby agreed.

"So nothing juicy happened?" I asked.

"I think Heidi wants to get back together with Nash," Abby said.

"I thought we weren't going to tell her," Ivy snapped.

"I know, but he doesn't like Heidi, so what's the difference?"

"It's okay," I said. "Maybe they are meant for each other."

"No way!" Ivy snapped again. "She's a tramp. And she's not you."

"And if you're not with Nash," Abby began, "then who are you meant for?"

I didn't answer. But I saw the image of Brandon staring down at me outside his guesthouse.

"If you don't know," Ivy asked, "then who does?"

I shrugged my shoulders.

"I know someone who will know," Abby said.

"Who?" Ivy and I asked in unison.

"Dr. Meadows," Abby said confidently. "She knows all."

FOUR

freaky fortunes

The last person I wanted to see was Dr. Meadows. I thought she'd been so eager to help Brandon find a cure for being a werewolf, only to discover that she'd been planning to exploit his condition. But Ivy and Abby were so excited to get their fortunes told again and reveal the whereabouts of my true love that they were successful in dragging me back to Penny for Your Thoughts.

"She might be ultrabusy," I said as we reached the storefront. Many cars were parked at the meters; we were lucky to have found a place. "It is the weekend."

"Stop being so negative," Ivy said. "We can wait."

"Yes, I'm totally geared up to see her!" Abby said, opening the door. "I can't wait to find out what she has to say about me. I mean, about Celeste."

"I just don't think I should be going in," I said. "Last time she gave me a freaky fortune and I got stuck in a snowstorm and was met by a pack of wolves."

"It's not supposed to snow and, believe me, this time I won't let you out of my sight," Ivy said in an overly protective tone. "You won't be seeing any wolves unless they are in the books she has for sale."

Abby pushed me inside. There were several customers looking at the holistic merchandise.

We wandered around the store, but Dr. Meadows wasn't at the counter to greet us. Instead we were met with the sounds of tribal drums over a gentle ocean surf and the scent of burning incense.

"Last time she was spot on!" Abby said, fingering a basket full of crystal rocks. "I wonder what she'll say about me this time."

Dr. Meadows was still nowhere in sight.

"Well, looks like she's busy in the back," I said. "Maybe we should go."

"What are you so afraid of? What could be so bad about her telling you you'll marry Nash?" Ivy asked.

I wasn't concerned about that—I felt I could choose my own romantic fate.

I was afraid Dr. Meadows would try to pump more info out of me than I would have expected to glean from her. However, maybe she thought I was pulling a prank when she found out the creature on video was a costumed hoax. I wasn't sure how she'd react.

Ivy held a pair of dangling blue crystal earrings, and Abby was examining amethyst bookends.

"I think these are really beautiful," Ivy said, holding her find up to one ear when Dr. Meadows came out from the back room and noticed us browsing through the store. She gave us a quick wave and rang up the other customers' purchases. When she was finished with them, we were her only other patrons. She greeted us with an inviting smile.

"Hello, girls." Dr. Meadows beamed happily. Her voice was soft and calming. Her long gray hair was in a ponytail and draped over one shoulder. Crystals and beaded jewelry tapped together like a wind chime. It seemed hard to think this woman wanted anything but the best for her customers. But I knew better.

"Hi, Dr. Meadows," Abby exclaimed like she was greeting her favorite aunt.

"Hello, Dr. Meadows," Ivy said eagerly.

I didn't say anything and pretended to be preoccupied with a book on massage. I didn't want to give any money to the psychic who was too quick to try to expose Brandon and only wound up giving attention to Nash's foolish prank. I also was wary of sipping her antioxidant tea. I wasn't sure what she might slip into my drink that might make me reveal the identity of the real werewolf.

But I think this private tea and face time with Dr.

Meadows was one of the reasons my friends wanted to come in the first place.

"What can I do for you today?" the mystic asked.

"We came here to see who is Celeste's true love," Abby said. "We think we know who it is, but we wanted to know your thoughts."

I knew who, but I wasn't giving my thoughts to anyone—especially in front of Dr. Meadows.

"I'd rather not have my reading done," I told her. "I'm not interested in finding out who I should be going out with," I said. "But please feel free to do readings for my friends."

Dr. Meadows led us into her inner sanctum. But she seemed keen on me. It was as if she was trying to get a vibe from me from across the darkened room.

"I'm sure, Celeste, that your reading will be fine," Dr. Meadows said with a gentle tone. "Just give me a chance."

"Come on," Abby said. "It'll be fun."

"That's why we're here," Ivy said.

"That's why you came," I mumbled softly so only she could hear.

"Fine, do mine!" Ivy said.

She hopped into the reading chair while Abby sipped her tea and I bit my tongue.

Dr. Meadows still gazed at me but then turned her attention to Ivy. Dr. Meadows took my friend's hand and closed her eyes. She took a deep breath in and exhaled.

"There are secrets that you want to know, but you may be the last to find out."

Dr. Meadows opened her purple shimmery lids and waited for Ivy's response.

"I didn't like that one," Ivy said, acting like her fortune was a pair of designer jeans that didn't fit. Dr. Meadows didn't offer a money-back guarantee, but that didn't stop Ivy from trying.

"I want another reading," she said. "I didn't like that one."

"A reading is a reading," Dr. Meadows said. "You can take it or leave it."

Ivy was in a huff. She frowned like a child.

Dr. Meadows saw a repeat customer, and she was smart enough to know that if Ivy left dissatisfied, it wouldn't be good for business. She took her hand again and Ivy's face lit up.

Dr. Meadows closed her eyes. "Friendship is as important to you as love. There will be an obstacle before you and a friend, but ultimately it will bring you closer together."

She turned to Abby. "What are you hiding?"

"I'm not hiding anything."

"Did you say something behind my back?" Ivy accused.

"No!"

"Girls." Dr. Meadows tried to appease them.

Ivy was still not pleased. "I still don't like it, Dr. Meadows."

In frustration, Dr. Meadows grasped her hand again. She closed her eyes and took a deep breath in and out.

"You will receive an unexpected gift," the psychic blurted out.

It seemed as cheesy a line as any handpicked message from a fortune cookie.

Ivy was ecstatic. "I knew it! See?"

She rose with a huge smile on her face and stood in front of Abby. "A present! I can't wait. And it isn't even my birthday!"

Abby returned her tea to the tea service, and Ivy took her seat.

Abby happily sat down and Dr. Meadows took her hand.

"Someone will confide in you and you must be sure to keep their confidence close to your heart."

"Ooh! Juicy!" Abby squealed.

Ivy looked perturbed. "You better tell me what they say!" Ivy said.

"What if it's you who tells me the secret?" Abby said.

"But I don't have anything to tell," Ivy said, thinking.

Abby was happy with her reading and didn't ask for a second or third.

"Now your turn, Celeste," Abby said. "Let's hear it. Will you marry Nash?"

"Ssh!" Ivy said. "You aren't supposed to say! Talk about keeping confidences? You just blew it!"

"I'm going to pass today," I said politely to Dr. Meadows. But Ivy and Abby dragged me out of my seat and sat me down in the reading chair.

"For you, today, it is free."

I tried to avoid eye contact with Dr. Meadows, but she grabbed my hand before I could go and closed her eyes. I was anxious about what she might say and would have covered my ears if only she wasn't holding my hands.

"Beware of a bite under a full moon. It will complicate your love life." I tried to pull away but her grip was fierce. Suddenly she let go.

I stood up, a little shaken.

As she rang up my friends' fortunes, I headed for the door.

"Wait, Celeste," Dr. Meadows called.

I stopped and reluctantly turned around.

The psychic came over to me and leaned in. "I was wondering—about the problem you were having last time? I'm still here to help."

I could see her hunger for paranormal information and felt a bit of sorrow for the holistic doctor. She had been correct about the readings she'd given me before but wrong about who the werewolf really was. I yearned for answers to Brandon's condition and anything that might help him. But his father would be coming to town and I trusted him more than her.

"I know your number," I said, and left before she could grab my hand again.

As we watched the Wolverines basketball game, Ivy and Abby were still hyper from their caffeine consumption and having new fortunes told.

I couldn't focus on the game, jotting down stories in my notebook or even daydreaming about Brandon. *Beware of a bite under a full moon. It will complicate your love life.* What had Dr. Meadows told me now? Would I be bitten, too, by a wolf? Or maybe by Brandon? I hadn't wanted my reading done in the first place. Her new words haunted me.

Apparently Ivy was distracted by her fortune, too.

"I can't wait until I get my present," Ivy mused. "I wonder who it will be from and what it will be."

"Well, someone is going to tell me something and I have to keep it a secret," Abby said as if her fortune were better.

"Not from me—" Ivy said.

"Yes, from you," Abby retorted. "Didn't you hear her?"

"But we tell each other everything." Ivy spoke forcibly.

"I know, but not this time." Abby swung her hair around with an attitude.

"I can't believe you." Ivy folded her arms and turned away.

"Dr. Meadows told me that's what would happen," Abby said, trying to console her.

"You have to tell me," Ivy ordered.

"I can't."

"But you have to," she insisted.

"I don't even know what it is!" Abby exclaimed.

I continued to stew over my reading. *Beware of a bite under a full moon . . .*

What did this mean? Who was going to be bitten? And

why would it affect my love life? Now I was afraid of a wolf bite—more than I had been before. Or maybe she meant metaphorically. Bitten by love?

"And what did yours mean?" Ivy asked, now turning back. "'A bite under a full moon'? Maybe Nash will give you a love bite!"

"Or maybe someone else will," Abby said.

"It has to be Nash," Ivy said.

"Dr. Meadows didn't say who it was. It could be anyone."

"Maybe it's Brandon!" Abby teased.

"Ooh!" Ivy said, making a face.

"He does have dreamy eyes," Abby said. "And he is kind of a hero."

"Just 'cause he found your dog doesn't mean he can replace Nash," Ivy barked. "Besides, he's a Westsider—"

Abby shook her head. "Dr. Meadows didn't say where her dream guy lived."

"She didn't even say it was going to be a guy. It could be an animal," Ivy said.

"Or a werewolf," Abby teased.

"Well, we don't know since she didn't say," Ivy said, resigned.

"C'mon, guys," I said. "I told you we shouldn't have gone to that psychic. She's just playing with our heads. She doesn't know what she's talking about."

"Then I'm not going to get an unexpected gift?" Ivy asked, upset.

Normally I would have laughed, but I was too consumed by my own fortune.

"Let's watch the game," Abby finally said.

I continued to hang out on the bleachers with my friends as they rooted for their boyfriends. Heidi Rosen cheered her heart out, waving her pom-poms at Nash when he scored.

"She makes me sick!" Ivy said. "Did you see that? She's a total tramp!"

"I really don't mind," I said.

"He likes you," Ivy said. "You know that."

I didn't want to think about Nash or continue to watch the game. I was exhausted from the fortunes and my imagination spinning out of control, wondering who or what was going to bite me. I grabbed my backpack and purse and rose.

"Don't leave," Abby said. "The game isn't over."

"You have fun," I said. "I'll call you guys later."

"This Heidi Rosen thing is really getting to Celeste," I heard Ivy say to Abby as I headed down the bleachers.

"Yes, we are going to have to fix it!" Abby said.

"Or fix Heidi!" Ivy declared as only a best friend would.

forecasts and flowers

My mind and heart were racing. Dr. Meadows's prediction haunted me like the other ones she had forecasted. Why did we have to go to Penny for Your Thoughts in the first place? Not only did I have to deal with Nash's behavior and Brandon's impending transformation but now another vague glimpse into my future? I wasn't sure what the prediction even meant. All I knew was someone was going to be bitten—by a wolf or werewolf—and somehow my love life would be complicated. Wasn't it complicated enough already?

Once I'd left the basketball game, I didn't know what to do. If I kept this a secret, I thought my mind would explode. Wasn't I holding too many secrets already? And if I was going to tell someone, there was only one person to tell. The only person I thought might understand was Brandon—but by telling him, I'd risk him withdrawing from me because I'd be causing him more stress than he already had. As I drove home, I contemplated this new dilemma and realized I had to tell Brandon. Not only was he a great friend, but he always seemed sensible and he might be able to figure out what Dr. Meadows meant. Besides, it might be important that he know what the psychic was saying about him. I dialed him on my cell, but he didn't pick up. When I pulled into my driveway, I texted him and waited. But still no response. Was he out in his backyard chopping wood? Or was he out grocery shopping for his grandparents and couldn't grab his ringing phone?

When I reached my bedroom, I heard "Fly Me to the Moon" playing. Finally!

"I need to see you," I blurted out.

"Are you okay?" he asked, his voice filled with concern.

"Yes. I just need to talk. Can I come to your house?"

"Uh . . . sure. I was just working out back, so I'll need to clean up."

"Well, that might have to wait. I saw Dr. Meadows again."

"Oh no," he said. Then he didn't speak.

"I'm on my way," I said, and hung up the phone.

I found Brandon outside his guesthouse, waiting for me and holding a bouquet of pink and yellow tulips. Not only wasn't he dirty from working, but his hair was slightly damp from showering, and he was wearing a different outfit from the one he'd worn to school.

When he saw me, he flashed a wide smile and handed me the lovely flowers.

"That's so sweet of you!" I said. "I love tulips!"

"I saw them at the market, and I thought they belonged with you," he said, watching me breathe them in. The fragrant aroma was as invigorating as he was. "I was planning on leaving them by your locker tomorrow, but when you called, I figured I'd give them to you in person."

"That was so thoughtful!" I leaned my head on his chest, but when I didn't come up for a kiss, he sensed something was wrong.

"What's up?" he asked.

"I don't want to tell you." I gazed down at my sneakers.

"Is everything all right?"

"For now."

"What do you mean?"

"I got another warning from Dr. Meadows," I said, now looking up at him.

"I thought you weren't going to see her."

"I wasn't. But Ivy and Abby got it in their heads that they wanted a fortune told—mine—and they dragged me there."

"Did you tell her about my condition? Did she have an antidote for me?" he asked, hopeful. I could tell that even though he didn't trust Dr. Meadows, either, he longed for a solution to his lycan transformation.

"I didn't ask. I was afraid if I said anything to her, then

she would somehow read my thoughts and figure out you were the werewolf. I didn't want her to show up at your house with a TV crew."

He sighed, disappointed, then pushed his dark locks away from his gorgeous face.

"I appreciate that," he said. "What did she say?"

"'Beware of a bite under a full moon. It will complicate your love life,'" I recited.

Brandon paused. At any moment he was going to confess he had dreams that he was going to bite me. But instead, he only laughed.

"You know it doesn't mean anything," he reassured me, resting his hand on my shoulder. "Why are you so worried?"

"But last time everything she said happened. 'Beware of the woods . . . of the sounds of howling.' Remember? 'There could be outsiders who will turn . . . underneath the glow of the full moon.' I was lost in the woods—and met that pack of wolves. And then you turned underneath the glow—"

"Of the full moon. I know. But just because she said it didn't mean it would happen. It could be coincidence," he tried to assure me.

"Yes. But when I left there, I got caught in a snowstorm, the full moon came out, you were bitten, and now you are a . . ."

He sighed. "It's okay."

"I don't know what it means." My hands shook and my voice quavered.

"What do you *think* it means?" he asked, entertaining my concern.

"That you will bite me and it will come between us."

"Now that is ridiculous! Have I bitten you before?"

"No."

"Then why would I now?"

"I don't know." I stared up at the most attractive guy I'd ever encountered, one who was not only handsome but kind. Then I realized I had just told him he might bite me and turn me into a wolfgirl. My love life was spinning out of control.

"Well, now you have me worried." He stepped away from me.

Getting it off my chest didn't relieve the burden of Dr. Meadows's warning like I thought it would; it only made things worse.

I bounced over to him—the guy who only a moment ago was sporting an infectious smile now was wearing a frown. "Like you told me," I began, "what she says can be baloney. And if it is true, well, who knows what it means? Maybe *I'll* bite *you*," I teased.

"I never figured moving here would be so complicated. So much has happened in such a short time. I figured the biggest thing I'd have to deal with was making friends. Now it seems like the last thing on my mind."

"And you should have friends. You should have me, Ivy, and Abby."

"I appreciate it—but like I said, that's the last thing I'm

concerned with now. I want to fix this situation so we can be together."

"I do, too."

"But now, with a prediction that I might bite you? The last person I'd ever want to hurt?"

I hated that I put that thought in Brandon's mind. My need for him to reassure me only made him the one who needed to be reassured now.

"You're right," I pressed. "You haven't bitten me before. In fact, you've been so gentle, I long for those nights when there is a full moon. If you were harmful, I wouldn't be standing here right now." I put my hand on his shoulder. "I didn't mean to come over here and add more stress to the situation. I came here to be with you."

I leaned into him and slid my hands around his back, still gripping my flowers. I clung to him as if I'd never let go.

He laid his head on my shoulder. I could feel his smooth cheek against my own and knew that by the next full moon his face would be ripe with facial hair and a goatee. This threat of his lycan condition was once again spoiling our moments together.

"Why don't we forget about things for a bit?" he asked, raising his head and taking a deep breath.

"Sure." I held the flowers close to me.

It was still chilly, but we walked up to the hilltop and hiked through the woods. Brandon was so stunningly gorgeous I couldn't take my eyes off of him. I had to squeeze his hands extra hard just to believe that this hot guy was indeed standing beside me. In the woods, alone, there was nothing that could come between us and no one we had to hide from. We could truly be ourselves. And even though Brandon wasn't in werewolf form, he had a heightened sense of our surroundings. He pointed to a pack of deer before they came into view. They were beautiful, hopping over branches and following one another in the woods.

Finally we rested at the foot of a tree by the stream. The water was cold but not frozen. It babbled so calmly that it was like the soothing sounds Dr. Meadows had playing in her store. It was wonderful to experience the sight of the flowing water in addition to the relaxing sounds of the stream.

Brandon pulled me to him. "Everything is so peaceful here," he said.

"I know. I wish we could stay forever."

"Let's," he said dreamily. "We'll set up a tent back here."

"And we'll live in it together."

"We'll make our own food and walk together during the day."

"We'd never get bored," I said.

"I don't think so, either. There would be so much to do. You could write your stories."

"And in the winter we could find a frozen pond where you could play hockey."

"We could be nature-schooled," he joked.

"Doesn't that sound awesome?" I said, resting my head on his leg.

Brandon fingered my hair, and I cozied up against him. Soon we were lost in each other's lips.

"I am really happy I came here," he said.

"To this stream?" I asked, dizzy from his kisses.

"No, to Legend's Run."

"Even with all its complications?"

"Well, I could do without some," he teased, "but yes, even with those."

"So you don't miss Miller's Glen?" I asked. "Not even a little bit? I can't imagine leaving my home and my friends."

"Yeah, I miss my friends. I was planning on going back for a visit, but I don't think so now—not with the whole moon-changing events."

"So you can't go back?"

"Not with an impending full moon."

I was relieved that he wasn't planning on leaving town anytime soon. But I also felt lonely for him—I was his only friend in Legend's Run. It only made me hug and kiss him more.

"Besides," he said, staring at me. "Nothing would take me away from you now. Not ever."

SIX

wolf calls

At school on Monday after the party fiasco, I found I was the subject of whispers and mumbling in the school hallways. Though Ivy and Abby were gossips and giggles as usual, Nash, his crew, and other students took Brandon's showing up to the party and leaving early—with me—as even more of a reason to isolate him. And my leaving with Brandon didn't go unnoticed by the other members of the once-happy sixsome.

I figured Nash wouldn't tell our friends that my reason for taking Brandon home had as much to do with my romantic feelings for him as it did my tendency to help out the underdog. Understandably, Nash wouldn't want to admit to our group that I was interested in anyone besides him.

As I met Ivy and Abby and pulled my books from my

locker, I noticed students laughing and pointing when they walked by a locker at the end of the first-floor corridor.

"What's up with that?" I asked Ivy and Abby.

"Don't know," Ivy said, almost salivating with interest. "Let's check it out."

We approached the small crowd and noticed it was Brandon's locker they were pointing to. It had the word WOLFMAN painted on it.

My heart sank. "This is awful!" I said.

"They aren't even original," Ivy added.

"Do you think Nash did this?" I asked.

"I don't think so . . . but let's ask him," Abby said. She stormed over to him and I followed closely.

Nash was standing by Heidi Rosen, and that made me even madder. If he was really so anxious to be with me again, he had a strange way of showing it.

I scooted past Abby and pushed my way between Nash and Heidi.

"Did you do that?" I asked him, point-blank.

"Do what?"

"Paint Brandon's locker."

"No. Why, does it need painting?"

"It does now." I was fuming.

Just then a crowd began to gather around us, not only Ivy and Abby but Jake and Dylan and a few more nosy members of the student body.

"If you didn't do this, then who did?" I asked.

"I don't know," he said. "Who am I, Sherlock Holmes?"

Heidi laughed an annoying cackle.

"Besides, we offered to take him home," Nash said. "Jake and Dylan, too. Wasn't that nice of us?"

"I think it was really nice," Heidi interjected. "He took me home."

I turned away and headed back to Brandon's locker.

"She's not even that athletic," Abby said, catching me at the locker. "She can't do a cartwheel, much less the splits. I don't know how she's a cheerleader."

"Yes," Ivy said, "and I guess you don't have to take an IQ test to get on the squad."

Even though deep down I wasn't truly jealous that Nash was hanging out with another girl, it was so nice to have my two friends defend me. I was hoping they'd do the same for Brandon.

"I have to go get some towels," I said.

"Why?" Ivy asked.

"I want to wipe this off."

"Celeste, you'll get dirty," she said. "Let the janitor take care of it."

"I don't want Brandon to see this. How would you feel if you got to your locker and someone had written WOLFMAN on it?"

Ivy thought. "That wouldn't make sense. I'm a girl."

But Abby got my point, and I think she still felt indebted

to Brandon for rescuing her dog because she said, "C'mon, Ivy, let's help."

She and Ivy followed me into the bathroom and grabbed paper towels and soaked half of them in soap and water. We returned to find Jake and Dylan standing by the locker, beaming.

Abby pushed them aside, and we started to wash the paint off.

"What are you doing?" Jake asked.

"What you should be doing," Ivy said.

"Are you crazy? Stop that."

He tried pulling his girlfriend away from the locker, but she refused.

"Get off," she said.

"You too," Dylan said to Abby. "Someone will see you."

"I think everyone sees us," she said, referring to the small crowd that had gathered around us.

"Why are you both defending him, too?" Jake asked. "It was wrong of you to bring another dude to the party. Don't you know how that looks?"

"I invited him," Abby said, putting some muscle into her scrubbing.

"Fine, you've done enough," Dylan said. "But you both are doting on him just as much as Celeste is."

"Are you crazy?" Abby asked. "We are so not."

"And what if they are?" I asked.

Just then I noticed Brandon walking down the hallway. A few howls came from the crowd.

Brandon looked slightly embarrassed and more than annoyed with the students' wolf cries. When he approached his locker, we were just finishing up.

"What's going on?" he asked, upset with what he saw.

"We were just cleaning lockers," I said. "It is part of our school renewal program."

"You girls don't have to," he said.

"We're almost done—" Abby said.

"You are done," Dylan directed.

"You too," Jake added. They took the towels from the girls and led them away from Brandon.

The crowd dispersed and I stood alone with Brandon, holding the blackened towel in my hand. My hair hung down in my face, and I had a few smudges on my sweater.

He gently lifted the piece of hair from my face and brushed it back. I felt a million chills surge through me. We locked eyes, and I was sure he was going to kiss me. Right there, in front of his locker, near meandering students, in full view of my friends.

The bell rang, and the hallway filled with students. Ivy came over to me and guided me back to our lockers. The last thing I was going to focus on was learning academics. There was only one thing I was going to think about and that was Brandon.

* * *

After a few more days of the wolf calls, I could see the harassment was taking its toll on Brandon. Though he tried to hide it, he seemed to be a bit agitated and almost depressed. I couldn't bear silent witness to it any longer.

"Where are you going?" Ivy asked when I didn't go in the direction of our table.

"I think we should sit somewhere else today," I said, trying for nonchalance. I acted like it wasn't a big deal to switch tables.

"What?" Ivy gasped. "This is our table. We've been sitting here for years!"

I spun around. "Why don't we all sit somewhere else?" I suggested as if I had a fabulous new idea. "It would be fun. A brand-new view of the cafeteria, and perhaps we could make new friends."

"We don't need new friends," she said in a huff.

"C'mon. Let's live on the edge. Just this once."

"I don't want to live on the edge," Ivy said. She shifted her hips to one side as if her tray were holding heavy textbooks instead of a small salad. "I want to sit with Jake."

"Yeah, and I want to sit with Dylan," Abby chimed in. "Don't you want to hang with Nash?"

"Listen," I began in a whisper. "If we sit with Brandon, whoever is doing this will stop tormenting him."

"Brandon?" they exclaimed in unison.

"That's what this is about?" Ivy wondered.

"I already invited him to my party," Abby winced. "Do

we have to eat lunch with him, too?"

"You guys are popular," I said. "So if we sit with him, he'll look cool because he's with the cool people. Then the spray-painting antics will be over."

"No, then they'll be spray painting our lockers as well," Ivy said.

"They wouldn't dare," I said. "That's why this is so easy—"

"Well, you're popular, too," Abby said. "Why don't you sit with him?"

They both glared at me with razor-sharp eyes, awaiting my answer.

This was the moment. I could either stand tall or cave in. Be the person I was hoping they'd be or behave as all the other cliques did and simply mind my own business. Ivy and Abby were going to sit by their boyfriends. Perhaps it was time for me to sit by mine.

"I think I will." The words came out before I had a chance to change my mind.

I thought Ivy was going to drop her tray from shock. "Oh, come on," she said. "Are you insane? You could be killed over there!"

"Yeah, it's totally not safe—or cool," Abby advised. "A party was one thing, but I agree with Dylan, we've done enough."

"I have to sit with Jake," Ivy said, "and Abby sits with Dylan and you with Nash. Let's go." They began to walk away, but I didn't follow.

"Are you coming?" Abby asked.

I didn't move. Instead I turned in the direction of Brandon's table—the skater table.

"Celeste!" Ivy called. But I didn't look back.

"C'mon, Celeste!" Abby said. "We get that you are trying to do the right thing."

But I didn't join my friends and continued to gaze toward the opposite side of the cafeteria.

"Fine." Ivy finally resigned. "We'll catch up to her after lunch."

"If she survives the lunch bell," Abby said. I could hear their heels clicking against the linoleum floor as they walked to our table.

At this point, I was no longer worried that my friends would abandon me. I knew they'd just assume I was up to my old goody-two-shoes save-the-world ways. And hadn't Brandon saved me from the wolves in the woods? This was the least I could do.

But it was harder than I thought. It would be the first time I sat anywhere else but with my friends. All my high school years were spent in Ivy's and Abby's company. Even if one was at home sick, I was by the side of the other. We never stepped foot on the other side of the cafeteria even to throw our trash away. And this time I was not only planning to venture onto their half but actually sit down with one of their own.

I took a deep breath and walked toward Brandon's table. At first I went unnoticed. But when I walked past several tables of Eastsiders and crossed into Westsider territory, I began to get stares. I was uncomfortable and my palms grew clammy, the tray beginning to slip and shake in my hand. The spoon for my Jell-O began to rattle, and it only drew attention to how nervous I felt inside. I knew it wasn't too late to turn back. No one would be the wiser. My friends would greet me with a laugh and a few "goody-girl" jabs. The Westsiders would go back to eating their sandwiches and talking about how materialistic we were.

But I remembered the stares from the wolves in the woods that day when the blizzard blinded me, I was lost, and Brandon saved me. These stares felt just as deadly, but I knew that I wasn't in any real physical danger now. I had to convince myself that Brandon was there for me—and I had to be there for him. I couldn't shy away from the unknown but needed to embrace it and have it provide me with strength, just as he had. I took another deep breath; I felt as if I were walking in the wrong part of town. This time I was the outsider, the one who didn't belong. But I didn't care. I stood tall and continued on my way, as if I'd been sitting on that side of the cafeteria since I was a freshman.

I came to the skater table, where Brandon normally sat. Several students eyed me but didn't say anything—as if my presence was too shocking for words. I set my shaking tray down on the table and I finally plopped down on the bench next to Brandon's empty seat. I heard several gasps and whispers.

"What is Miss Priss doing here?" Hayley said loud enough for me to hear. Her friends laughed.

I ignored her.

"Don't you have your own table over there on the East-side?" she asked.

As I opened my lunch, I felt unsettled and understood the loneliness Brandon must have felt eating by himself. The caf was filled with noisy laughing, talking, and eating. Everyone had a pal, a best friend, or a group to chill out with. Not being included or having anyone to even smile at made me feel very self-conscious and hollow inside.

And then it hit me. What if Brandon didn't eat in the lunchroom today? What would I do? Would I sit and eat alone the entire lunch bell—or get up to leave early to jeers and howling from Westsiders who thought, to begin with, that my presence must be a joke? I didn't want to become the laughingstock of Legend's Run. The last thing I felt like doing was eating my lunch—my stomach was flip-flopping with nerves—but I knew I had to do something other than sit and stare back at the glaring eyeballs.

My sandwich felt rotten as it hit the pit of my stomach, but I continued to chew and swallow another bite. Finally I spotted Brandon coming into the lunchroom.

I breathed a sigh of relief.

Brandon caught sight of me and appeared just as shocked

as the others. But instead of making remarks and scowling, his face brightened. He headed over with all lunchroom eyes on him and sat down next to me.

"What are you doing here?" he asked with a smooth, sultry voice.

"I was tired of watching you get teased. Now maybe it will stop."

He glanced around. Everyone was looking at us, especially my friends at my table, but I continued to eat my lunch as if we were the only ones in the lunchroom.

Brandon didn't know what to do. It wasn't the reaction I'd expected.

"It's okay," I said. "You can eat, too."

"Did you tell your friends about us?" he whispered.

"No."

"Then what's up?" he asked. "Why the sudden change in seating?"

"I wanted Ivy, Abby, and me to sit with you. If everyone saw us hanging out with you, then I thought . . ."

"The hazing would stop?"

"I thought it might."

"But Ivy and Abby didn't go for it?" he said with a smile. I shook my head.

"That's really cool."

"That they didn't?"

"No, that you did. That was really cool." He locked eyes with me.

I could kiss you right now, his gaze spoke to me. I blushed and turned to my food.

He opened his bag and pulled out two overstuffed sandwiches. Ever since Brandon had become a werewolf, his eating habits had taken on a new life. He ate three times the normal amount of food a typical student would eat.

He scooted his leg next to mine so they were touching. No one in the cafeteria knew our little secret. I was tingly and so distracted that I could barely eat my lunch.

I was hoping we'd be able to get through lunch without incident, but deep down I knew that wasn't going to happen.

Nash approached the table and stood across from me and Brandon. Jake and Dylan flanked him on either side.

"What's up, Wolfie?" Nash said.

"Nash, please," I said.

"Just wanted to see what the Wolfman eats for lunch. Deer meat? Or are you a vegan werewolf?"

"Stop it, Nash."

"Have to get a girl to fight your battles?" Nash said coldly.

Brandon tensed up. "You mean your girl?" he muttered under his breath.

"What did you say?" Nash asked.

"Celeste is welcome to sit wherever she likes," Brandon said. "I don't own her, and neither do you."

"Listen, bud," Nash said, leaning in so only Brandon and I could hear. "I know what I saw that night. I can turn you in to the zoo sooner rather than later."

Brandon leaned in, too. "Well, if you do believe you saw something, then you better watch your back. A full moon is coming."

For a moment they continued to stare at each other, like two wolves ready for a fight.

"Stop it—both of you," I finally said.

Mrs. Dent, our lunchroom monitor, must have noticed the rising tensions and came over to our table.

"Is everything all right here?" she asked.

"Uh . . . yes," Nash said. "I was just making sure our friend here had enough to eat."

"Well, the lunch period is almost over," she said.

"We were just leaving," my former boyfriend replied.

Before he left, Nash shot me a cold stare that chilled my veins. Dylan and Jake followed him back to my friends' table.

"I guess this wasn't a good idea," I said, frustrated with myself. "The bullying didn't stop. I might have made it worse. I thought I was doing the right thing."

"You were," Brandon said, squeezing my knee. "You were."

The bell rang, and I threw my remaining lunch in the trash. I hadn't been able to eat much. I'd have to wait until after school to have a snack. But if my stomach still felt as upset as it was now, I wouldn't have much of an appetite then, either.

Ivy caught up to me by the cafeteria exit and took me by the hand, leading me away from Brandon.

"Okay, community service time is over," she said as she yanked me into the crowd of students leaving the lunchroom.

When fifth bell was finally over, Nash was waiting for me outside my classroom.

"What was that about?" he asked, sliding up close to me. "Are you trying to embarrass me?"

"You mean lunch?" I asked.

"Uh . . . yeah. I know we aren't back together, but are you trying to play a trick on me?"

"Of course not, Nash," I said sincerely. "I wanted to show solidarity. That whoever is tormenting him—it needs to stop."

"You think it's me," he said as if he was genuinely hurt.

"No. You said you didn't write that on his Jeep and I believe you. But that means someone else did. So I'm doing it to stop them."

He shook his head at me in frustration.

"What?" I said. "I'd do the same for you—only you don't need it. You are popular and everyone in school loves you."

"I know. I know you'd do the same for me. That's why you are so cool."

I was thrilled by Nash's compliment. It was weird feeling I understood him more than the other girls at Legend's Run. And that he in turn saw me differently, too.

"I guess I just wish this time that I was the new kid in school—that you wanted to sit with me," he confessed as students walked by.

Nash's admission went straight to my heart. For a moment, he wasn't masking himself with the bravado of a high school jock but rather letting me into his soul.

"Well, it didn't seem to work as well as I'd like. I might have caused Brandon more trouble. I'll be returning to our table tomorrow."

Nash turned serious. "Uh . . . things might be different there, too."

"What do you mean?"

"You put me in a bind—in front of our friends and the whole school. I now know you were doing what you thought was right—but it looks like you left me for Brandon—a West-sider, no less." He shook his head again in frustration. "Maybe I need to show you what you are really missing by making the choices you are making. By choosing the wrong side. But mostly the wrong guy." Nash's voice wasn't threatening but rather low and sultry. And his expression was soft and sincere. If he'd been this attentive before, perhaps we'd be together now.

Nash was fighting for me as much out of pride as for the deep and true feelings I sensed he had for me. There was a slight part of me that was attracted to that—as much I'd been attracted to him in the first place. But as Nash smiled and walked away, I realized that Brandon didn't have to change to be the guy I loved. He already was that way, naturally.

The following day, when the lunch bell rang, I wasn't sure which table I should sit at. If I sat with Brandon, there would be more confrontation, and if I sat with my friends, Nash would feel that he won his battle.

As I walked into the lunchroom with Ivy and Abby, I wondered what Nash had planned to convince me I was making the wrong choices in guys. I wasn't expecting flowers or a ring, but I was wondering what the handsome jock had in mind. I was also slightly nervous that he would use Brandon's lycan identity in hopes of getting my clique on his side. It was then I saw Nash already hanging out at our table—with his arm around Heidi Rosen. Before I knew it, she sat down in my spot—the seat that I'd been sitting in since freshman year.

I was being replaced by Heidi Rosen? He hadn't told my friends about Brandon being a werewolf. Instead he was doing something strong to let me know what I was missing being without him. Though we'd been on and off before, Nash didn't ever have a girlfriend that he'd brought to our table.

Ivy noticed Heidi, too. "What is she doing in your seat?"

"We'll get to the bottom of this," Abby said.

My best friends stormed over to our table and faced Nash.

"That's Celeste's seat," Abby said.

"But she's not sitting here anymore," he said.

"Uh . . . yes, she is," Ivy said.

"Then she can sit there," he said, pointing to the empty space on the other side of Heidi. "You know how she likes to make new friends."

My two friends stormed back to me. "She won't budge,"

Ivy said. "Maybe if we had a crane—"

"Or a pack of cigarettes," Abby said. "I get secondhand smoke just from looking at her."

"It's okay," I said. Since I really liked Brandon, it wasn't my place to make a fuss about Nash hanging out with another girl.

"I can't believe him," Abby said. "He must really be jealous that you were kind to Brandon."

"He invited her to sit with us," Ivy said. "He didn't ask us, she just sat down, right in the spot that is yours! I know I'm going to lose my lunch."

"She's all about herself," Abby said. "Just like every other girl he dates. Except you. Don't you see that's why you belong together?"

"It's all right," I said. "I'll sit somewhere else."

"But you can't. You'll sit next to me and Dylan," Abby offered.

"No," Ivy interjected. "By me and Jake."

"I suggested it first," Abby said.

"But Celeste might want to sit with us, too," Ivy said to Abby as if I wasn't standing there. "We'll let her decide."

My friends looked to me to make a choice between them, putting me more on the spot than I already was.

I didn't mind so much being the odd girl out, but I did mind having my spot taken in such a brazen manner. I wasn't in the mood to fight, and I didn't want to use Brandon as a weapon and eat with him to get back at Nash.

"Thanks. You both are the best," I said truthfully. "But I think I want to eat alone."

"You have to eat with us," Ivy said. "We've eaten together for years!"

"Yes, this is your table," Abby said. "I don't mind getting in his face for real this time," she offered.

But that was what Nash wanted. He wanted to be fought over. I could have hung out at the table with them and shown him that it didn't upset me, but I was too tired. By sitting with Brandon yesterday, I was trying to show anyone who was bothering him that he did have friends—even if it was only me. But today, Nash was trying to get back at me. And he'd think he won—even if it was a contest that I wasn't really participating in.

"You can't sit with another guy at a table in front of the whole school without Nash getting worked up," Ivy said.

"I was just trying to help—" I began.

"We know. But that's not what it looked like to him," she added.

I couldn't sit at our table with Heidi Rosen sitting in my seat. And I wasn't in the mood to march over and demand that she sit somewhere else. "It would be too awkward," I said. "But I also can't sit with Brandon. I've caused him enough trouble."

"I'd sit with you somewhere else," Abby said, "but I'd like to hang out with Dylan. I haven't seen him all day."

"I understand," I said. Although I wasn't sure if I did. I

hadn't eaten with my true love the last few months so I could avoid turmoil with my friends. My friends couldn't miss a day for me?

Ivy didn't say anything. She didn't have to.

"It's okay," I said to her. "I'll see you after lunch."

"You have to eat with us!" she begged. "It's what Nash really wants."

"Why do I have to do everything for Nash?" I asked.

Ivy was hurt. "Everything is changing!" she exclaimed as if her world were crumbling down around her. "You have to stop being Mother Teresa."

I didn't understand this whole clique mentality. If I had my way, everyone in the school would just sit at one big table.

"Where are you going to eat?" she asked, worried.

"I may just go to the library and read. I'm not very hungry anyway."

I was upset. I wasn't sitting next to Brandon to get back at Nash or to prove anything to him; I was doing it to show Brandon support. But Nash was striking back in a big way by inviting Heidi Rosen to sit in my seat at our table. I was stung with jealousy, not so much about Nash, but about my friends, as I headed out of the cafeteria and saw Heidi across from Ivy and Abby. Were my best friends going to replace me, too?

I longed to sit next to Brandon, like yesterday when I got to have my leg and ankle touch his. Maybe if he was smooth enough, Brandon would grab my hand underneath the table. I imagined us all together, Ivy and Jake, Abby and Dylan, and me and Brandon. He would be a star to them, joining us at campfires on his hilltop, hiking, and skating on his frozen pond. And when he turned into were-form he'd be the handsome and heroic member of our group. But was I open enough to have Nash bring along Heidi? We girls were a threesome, and I'm not sure that I was ready for Ivy and Abby to have a new best friend.

But though it would be awkward, I think I was ready—because I was in love with Brandon. And having Brandon included definitely trumped my jealousy for seeing my former boyfriend cozy with a hot girl.

"You want everyone to get along," Ivy said. "But unfortunately that's not how the this town works. You have to sit with us tomorrow. You have to. Our friendship depends on it."

But even I had my limits. "I can't. Not with Heidi, too."

I took my lunch and exited the cafeteria, not passing Brandon along the way. I found an empty alcove on the lower level and sat down. I wasn't even in the mood to eat, but I did feel a sense of relief having a peaceful moment to myself. I took out a book and began to escape into its pages.

With the full moon approaching and Brandon's impending transformation coming, I wasn't sure what other changes were going to happen as well. Would I continue to sit alone and be pushed out of the clique I'd been part of for so many years? Would Brandon be bullied now more than ever because I showed him my support? And would others besides Nash find out that Brandon was the one howling in the full moon-light?

It was too much for me to grapple with alone during a single lunch period. And for the first time at Legend's Run High, I wanted to spend time by myself. Ivy was correct. Things were changing. And one of those things was me.

father's arrival

It was in the late afternoon one day before the rise of the full moon when I found myself sitting with Brandon and his grandparents on their living room couch, awaiting Dr. Maddox's arrival.

I was excited to meet Brandon's father. His visit would not only offer Brandon reassurance by his father's presence, but Dr. Maddox might even have an idea for a possible cure.

Brandon, his legs twitching restlessly, kept switching channels on the TV.

"It's okay," I said. "He'll be here soon."

But that didn't seem to assuage his agitation.

Even his husky began to bark as if he, too, was feeling Brandon's tension.

"Calm down, Apollo," he commanded. Instantly the dog winced, then lay by Brandon's feet.

"Why are you so antsy?" I asked. "I bet you are excited to see your dad."

Brandon didn't respond but perked up. At the same time, Apollo's ears stood up, and he raced to the window and began barking.

Within a few seconds there was a knock on the door.

I half expected Dr. Maddox to enter in a lab coat, wearing thick black glasses, and mad scientist–style gray, wiry, untamed hair. But instead he was handsome like Brandon, with dark hair, and dressed in a brown sport coat, jeans, and trendy metal rectangular-shaped glasses.

"Connor, it's so wonderful to see you!" Brandon's grandmother gushed.

Dr. Maddox was greeted by hugs and kisses from his delighted parents. It was obvious he was thrilled to see Brandon as he gave him a warm embrace.

"Dad, this is Celeste," Brandon said proudly as if he was showing me off. I didn't know if Brandon had even mentioned me to his dad—or what he might have said about our relationship. I felt awkward not knowing but reassured that Brandon seemed so happy.

"Hello there, Celeste," Dr. Maddox said, extending his hand. "I am very pleased to meet you."

"I'm pleased to meet you, too, Dr. Maddox." I shook

the senior Maddox's hand. It was firm and warm, just like Brandon's.

"Please, call me Connor," he said, and gestured for us all to sit down.

I sat quietly and watched the Maddox family reunite as Dr. Maddox shared a few tales from overseas. It was interesting to see the dynamics of Brandon's family. They all seemed very intelligent and motivated. And Brandon beamed, having his father and grandparents surrounding him. It was the first time I'd seen him truly relaxed.

"Well, it's time for us to turn in," his grandparents said when the evening wore on.

We all said our goodnights to them. I felt the mood shift a bit and realized that now was the time that Brandon needed to tell his father why he'd asked him to come home from Europe.

Dr. Maddox checked to see that his parents were out of earshot, then he sat across from us in a comfy chair while Brandon and I sat close on the sofa.

"So, what did you want to tell me?" Dr. Maddox said. "You two aren't getting married, are you?" he joked.

"No." Brandon laughed.

"Then what is it that you wouldn't tell me on the phone?"

"I was bitten by a wolf."

Dr. Maddox was taken aback. "Are you okay?"

Brandon pulled off his fingerless glove and showed his

scarred palm to his father.

He examined it closely. "When did this happen?"

"A few months ago."

"Where?"

"In a wooded area."

"What were you doing in the woods?" his father asked.

"He saved me," I blurted out. "It was my fault. I was in the woods—lost—and stumbled on a pack of wolves. I'm sure I wouldn't be here if it weren't for Brandon. He is a hero."

Brandon blushed, and Dr. Maddox beamed with pride.

"Why didn't you tell me this when it happened?" his father asked.

Brandon withdrew his hand and replaced the glove. "I didn't want to bother you."

"You aren't a bother. You should have called me. I want to know what is going on with you. Just because I'm in Europe doesn't mean I'm not your father," Dr. Maddox said sincerely. "Did you go to a doctor?"

"Not at first. But Grandma saw my hand and made me go. I got a shot and some stitches and that was the end of that."

"Or so we thought," I said.

Dr. Maddox raised an eyebrow over his glasses. "So you said you had a reaction to something. Is this what it was?"

"Yes," Brandon said.

"What kind of reaction did you have? A fever?"

"Yes. But it didn't happen until a month later."

"Then how do you know it was from the bite?" his father wondered.

"You'll think I'm crazy."

I looked to Brandon.

"Tell me," his father persuaded. "I'm sure I've heard something like it before. It's hard to surprise a scientist."

"Something happened." Brandon wrung his fingers together nervously.

"What, Brandon? I'm here to listen."

"I changed." Brandon fidgeted in his seat.

"Changed how?"

"It was a full moon when I was bitten. Then the following full moon, I got the fever." Brandon paused. I placed my hand on his knee, trying to give the comfort I think he was searching for. "I had these dreams all month long," he continued. "Weird ones." Brandon turned back to me.

"You have to tell him everything," I coaxed him.

"You'll think I'm crazy, Dad."

"I won't," he said reassuringly, with a bit of impatience and weariness from his long day of traveling. "Go on."

"This is hard to talk about."

"They were just dreams, right?" his father asked. "Everyone has weird dreams. It's okay."

"I was a wolf. Running through the woods and fields. Even around houses."

That part shocked me. I hadn't heard that Brandon had dreamed about being near homes, too.

"Anything else?" his father asked.

"I couldn't sleep. I mean, I dreamed, but I didn't feel like I was really sleeping. I woke up exhausted and starved."

It was apparent his father was concerned for his son as he leaned in to hear more. "I wish you would have talked to me," Dr. Maddox said.

"What was there to tell?" Brandon said. "'I've been having nightmares, so come home from Europe?' I'm not a kid."

"I know—but . . . so what is this concern with the full moon? You've never been into that sort of cosmic stuff before."

"One night Celeste came over, and we were hanging out in the guesthouse," Brandon continued. "The sun set and I felt strange. . . . I really don't want to tell you more."

Brandon stopped and covered his face with his hands.

It was like he was afraid of revealing actions that might make the doctor think he should be institutionalized.

"You'll think I'm making this up," he started again. "It's nuts. This stuff doesn't really happen—just in movies."

"Well, Celeste seems like a very smart girl, and she's sitting with you and seems to believe in you," his father said. "And you've never lied to me before—why would I think you're lying to me now?"

"Because I turned into a werewolf!" Brandon exclaimed, his hands tightening into fists.

His father's eyes widened and his mouth dropped open. Then he laughed. "You've got to be kidding me!"

"I'm not." Brandon was dead serious.

"You are paying me back for disrupting your life. I understand that."

"I'm not, Dad."

"All you had to do was say you wanted me to come back for a visit. I would have. You didn't have to concoct this crazy story."

"I knew you'd think I was crazy."

"That is the strangest thing you've ever said. Even as a kid. I thought it was something serious. Now I can breathe easier."

His father stretched his arms out and sighed. Then he placed his hands on his lap as if he was signaling the end of the conversation. "We can talk more tomorrow. I'm sure I'll have some dreams, too, tonight. Maybe I'll be a zombie."

When Dr. Maddox stood up, I saw all the hope rush out of Brandon. I knew I had to say something before his father went up to bed.

I rose with all the force I had. "It wasn't just a dream, Dr. Maddox," I said, my voice quaking and my eyes almost teary. "It really happened. I saw it. I was there."

He stopped and studied me as if he didn't know how to address my sudden outburst.

"You have to believe me," I pleaded. "Us. I mean, Brandon."

Dr. Maddox was in disbelief. I wasn't sure what he was going to do—and it seemed, as he stared at us, that he didn't know what to do himself.

"See—I was afraid you wouldn't believe me," Brandon said sadly. "If I can't trust you—who can I trust?" He got up and started for the back door.

"Brandon, get back here," his father called.

But instead Brandon headed outside. The screen door slammed behind him.

Tears welled in my eyes. I felt awful for Brandon. And bad for his father.

"Celeste—" his father said, stopping me. "What is he really going through? Is he having a hard time adjusting here?"

"Brandon needs your help," I urged him. "Tomorrow is a full moon."

"I'm not sure—"

"Please, Dr. Maddox. If he knows you don't believe him, you'll break his spirit."

"That is why he insisted that I come here now?"

"Yes. Tomorrow is a full moon," I repeated. "You will see the change for yourself."

Dr. Maddox wasn't convinced. "Well, whatever this is, I'm not leaving. We'll get this solved. Okay?"

We found Brandon outside, throwing rocks between the trees.

"I shouldn't have asked you to come," he told his father.

It was as if those words hit his father like an arrow. I could see the pain in his eyes—the pain of not being there for his son, even now that he was in fact physically here.

"No. You were right to." He patted Brandon on the shoulder. "It's been a long day for both of us. We'll get some rest. Tomorrow I'll take some samples, take a look, and run some tests. And by sunset we'll see what happens." Dr. Maddox was more confident than concerned.

Brandon's sullen mood brightened. "You will?"

"You are my son," he said. "I won't let anything happen to you now that I'm here."

Brandon's father gave him a reassuring hug.

"It was great meeting you, Celeste. I'm grateful Brandon has found such a good friend."

Dr. Maddox headed back inside, and Brandon took my hand and walked me to my car.

"I feel so stupid," he said.

"Don't. He has to know."

"Maybe I should have gone to Dr. Meadows instead. She's into the paranormal. My dad is a scientist. Something like this is only fantasy to him."

"He'll see tomorrow night how fantasy is reality."

Brandon looked up at the almost-full moon. Tomorrow evening would be the first of his three nightly transformations.

He hugged me hard. I could feel the weight of his condition wearing on him.

But I was curious about one part of his dreams that I hadn't heard before. "When you've been dreaming about running around houses," I asked, "where were you going?"

"To yours," he said. "Always to yours."

Brandon kissed me goodnight and watched me as I pulled away. I wasn't going to get much sleep tonight, and neither was Brandon. And Dr. Maddox was in for a restless night as well.

EIGHT

turning

I stewed all day at school in anticipation of Brandon's transformation and Dr. Maddox's reaction.

When I saw Brandon getting into his Jeep at the end of the day, I said good-bye to Ivy and Abby and got into my car. I didn't want to miss a thing now with Dr. Maddox in town.

Brandon gave me a quick kiss when I parked next to him at his grandparents' house. We went inside and found Dr. Maddox in the basement. It was unfinished, without carpeting, a TV, or an office. Instead, it had an old Ping-Pong table with boxes piled on top, a washer and dryer, and a bathroom. He was toiling with a small chest with petri dishes, beakers, and microscope.

"It's like a museum down here," his father said. "All my dreams and early science projects. When I was young and watched monster movies, I always wanted to create a Frankenstein monster and cure a werewolf. I didn't know that all these years later, I might have to for real."

We made our way back up the wooden stairs and into the kitchen. Brandon sat down at the table while his father opened a bag.

"Uh . . . what are you going to do?" Brandon asked.

"Take a blood sample."

That was something the mystic Dr. Meadows wouldn't have done.

"Is that okay with you?" his father asked.

"Whatever you have to do to cure me," Brandon said.

We sat in the kitchen while Brandon's father prepared to take a sample of Brandon's blood. I wasn't normally squeamish, and if I was going to be a nurse like I hoped, I'd have to be doing this myself one day. I watched closely as Dr. Maddox washed his hands and applied a rubber tourniquet to Brandon's upper arm. He made Brandon squeeze a rubber ball in his hand and quickly found a prominent vein.

"How was school today?" he asked matter-of-factly as he opened an alcohol prep swab and wiped an area on the inside of Brandon's arm. He unwrapped a small butterfly needle and attached it to a plastic vial.

"It was okay," Brandon said.

Brandon must have noticed my eager expression leaning in on the kitchen table and watching Dr. Maddox like I was a nurse in training.

"Want one, too?" Brandon asked.

"No, I just find this fascinating."

"You want to be in the medical field?" Dr. Maddox asked.

"I've thought about becoming a nurse. I like helping people."

"You'll just feel a little prick," he said to Brandon.

Dr. Maddox stuck the needle in Brandon's vein and removed the tourniquet and ball.

"So, do you two have any classes together?" Dr. Maddox asked as he filled the plastic vial and removed the syringe. He put a piece of gauze on Brandon's arm and asked him to hold it.

"Yes," Brandon said. "But I don't learn much in those classes. Celeste is a distraction."

The two of them laughed, and my face flushed.

Brandon's father placed a sample on a slide and then marked the tube and put it in a plastic bag. He dusted off one of the microscopes he'd brought up from the basement and placed the slide with the blood sample in it.

In chemistry class we looked at slides. I remembered I had lowered the microscope a little too far and it crashed into the slide and broke it. A few other students did that day, too, and we all had to pay a small replacement fee.

"Hmm . . ." his father said. "Interesting."

Then his father took a pair of tweezers. "This may hurt."

"Like the blood draw didn't?" Brandon said.

He plucked a few strands of hair from Brandon's head.

"Ouch!" he yelled.

He plucked a few more from his son's arm. He put those in another plastic bag and marked them.

He examined a strand under the microscope. "Hmm . . ." he said again. "This, too, is very interesting."

"What?" Brandon said. "What is it?"

"I haven't seen anything like this before," his father said. "It's very odd."

His father was preoccupied. He appeared perplexed and made a few notes into his phone.

"Perhaps I am wrong," he continued. "I'll have to send this off for further testing."

Dr. Maddox told us to hang out in Brandon's guesthouse as he stayed in the main house and made some calls.

Brandon was relieved that his father was here but worried at the same time.

"It's okay," I said. "Now he can find you a cure."

"I don't know. I still think I should have talked to Dr. Meadows instead. The look on my dad's face . . . He could be doing important work and instead he's here trying to help me."

That's one of the reasons I cared for Brandon so much. He was handsome, which didn't hurt, but his heart was just as beautiful.

"I'm sure his work can wait. And besides, this is important. You're his son, don't forget."

Brandon gazed out the window. It was still light out, and the moon was partially covered by a few passing clouds.

"Wouldn't it be cool," Brandon said, "if he could find an

antidote? Then I wouldn't have to worry about the moon—only about getting Ivy and Abby to sit on my side of the cafeteria."

"I think it might be easier to be a werewolf," I said, and we both laughed.

I hugged him and let myself completely relax into the embrace. Brandon had just leaned in to kiss me when his father knocked on the door.

"Come in," Brandon said as we both sat up.

"I've made some calls," Brandon's father said. "I'll send the samples off to one of our labs."

Brandon and I were relieved. I reached my hands in the air.

"Yay!" I said. "I knew you could do it!"

Just then I noticed that the inside of the room was becoming lighter than the outside.

"The sun is setting," I said, peering out the window.

Dr. Maddox appeared nervous. He pulled back the curtains and stared up at the moon.

"We have to get outside," Brandon said.

"So, do you feel any different yet?" his father asked.

"I need to be outside," Brandon repeated vehemently.

"Now, let's remain calm. If something is really going to happen, it's best if we stay in a controlled setting," his father said.

"I'm burning up!" Brandon said.

"It's starting. . . ." I told his father.

Dr. Maddox watched his son with minor skepticism. Even though he had just seen something unusual under the microscope, I suspected he wasn't ready to accept anything else unusual.

Brandon pulled his shirt off over his head. "It's barely warm in here," his father said. "I don't think you should—"

Brandon pushed past his father. "I don't want you to see me like this."

"I have to know what's happening so I can help you."

"I can't! I'm burning up!" Brandon grabbed the handle of the door for support, and when he got his bearings he opened it.

"Brandon, wait!" his father said.

Brandon bolted out of the guesthouse. He threw off his shoes and socks and ran up the hill.

"Brandon, what are you doing?" Dr. Maddox hollered.

We began chasing after him as he ran farther into the woods. His strength and speed were beyond his father's and mine. We couldn't keep up. It was then we heard a howl in the distance.

We found Brandon in the shadows by a tree. He wasn't out of breath but rather out of spirit. He was lonely, running from the two people he cared about the most.

"Brandon?" his father called.

Brandon didn't move.

"I need to see you. Come here. Why did you run off?" His father stepped closer. We heard a low growl.

"I think an animal is near him," Dr. Maddox said. "Brandon, be careful. It's dark. You might run into something."

"Brandon," I called. "It's me, Celeste. We want to help you."

Brandon still didn't move. We could hear heavy breathing.

"Brandon—I need to see you." His father took another step.

Brandon emerged from the shadows. The moonlight cast a glow on him. His usually blue eyes were intensely gray and his physique was transformed. He had light brown hair on his chest and face, and the fangs of a wolf were piercing through the break in his lips.

His father drew back.

"Oh my—" he gasped. "Brandon?"

Brandon just stood by the tree, still breathing heavily.

"Brandon—is that you?"

Brandon didn't move or answer.

"I didn't believe it at first, either," I said, relieved to finally have someone else witness the event who could possibly help.

Dr. Maddox was amazed to see his son transformed. "I can't believe it," he said. "Even though I'm seeing it with my own eyes."

Brandon didn't say anything.

"I am a scientist," Dr. Maddox said, breathless. "I had to have proof. And I think we have it." But then Dr. Maddox's fascination turned to concern. He was wary around his son. "Step back," he warned me. "He could attack at any moment."

"No," I said. "He won't. He's not like that."

"Celeste, it's for your own good. Please, we can't be so sure."

"I am. I've seen him before."

"I'll have to take more samples," his father said. He had brought his bag with a syringe.

But there were no tests for what Brandon was experiencing emotionally. His own father was afraid of him.

Brandon bared his fangs and growled. He held his hand out to keep his father at bay.

"It's okay," said Dr. Maddox. "It will only take a second."

"I don't think he wants you to," I warned.

"But I have to."

Brandon growled again.

"Celeste, you must leave."

"But—"

His father's expression was filled with fear and concern. "You can't be around him," he demanded.

"I have before. Many times," I tried to explain to him.

"Brandon could be dangerous."

Brandon's intense gray eyes softened, as if he was saddened by his father's remark.

"But he's not." I defended Brandon. "He's not."

Brandon saw his father step toward him with the syringe.

"It might only be a matter of time," his father said.

As his father drew closer, Brandon's chest heaved.

"Don't—" I said. "He doesn't want you to—"

Just then Brandon let out a maddening howl so fierce his father dropped the syringe.

Brandon growled and clenched his fists and disappeared into the night.

We waited for a moment, but I knew Brandon wasn't going to return.

"You must promise me," Dr. Maddox said forcibly. "You must not see him again."

"But—I have to—"

"It's impossible. Not with my son like this."

I couldn't believe what was happening.

"You must promise me not to see him during a full moon. You saw—my son is a dangerous creature!"

"But he's not," I said. "He's not dangerous! You have to believe us!"

Dr. Maddox quickly escorted me back down the hill in silence. He was determined to get me out of the area.

He and Brandon were alike—they were both protective. I knew in Dr. Maddox's mind he was rescuing me from a dangerous situation. But I knew better. Brandon could be dangerous, but he wasn't—especially not to me.

I couldn't disobey Dr. Maddox's orders. He was protecting me out of the goodness of his heart and though it pained me to see him react to Brandon in this way, I didn't have a chance to convince him otherwise. If I raised too much of a fuss, Brandon's grandparents would be alerted, and I knew he didn't want them to know about his condition.

Even through his trendy rectangular-shaped glasses, his eyes shone wide with fear. I reluctantly got into my car, and Dr. Maddox shut the door for me. He waited as I started the engine.

As I pulled away from Brandon's guesthouse, a maddening howl rained down from the hilltop like an animal crying out in pain.

That night I felt ill. I was hoping Brandon would come to me in the night, show up outside, throw rocks at my window, or call me—anything to let me know how he was doing. But he didn't. I needed him to reassure me that he was okay, just as much as Dr. Maddox wanted to ensure I was safe.

I know it had to be shocking for Dr. Maddox to see his son in a paranormal condition. I had been shocked at first, too, and it took me quite a while to understand that I had truly witnessed Brandon become a werewolf and that it wasn't a dream. And inevitably I was drawn to Brandon, not repelled or frightened. Did Brandon have a different energy around his father, or was Dr. Maddox's own fear keeping him away?

Then I thought about Dr. Meadows's warning—*Beware of a bite under a full moon. It will complicate your love life.* What did it mean exactly? Was Dr. Maddox saving me from being bitten by Brandon? And how could he have known about the psychic's prediction?

Dr. Meadows had her own reasons to want to see Brandon—she sought fame and fortune—while Dr. Maddox now sought to keep us apart. He feared his own son.

I had proof that Brandon was benevolent: me. I'd never had a scratch, a wound, or any harm from being with him in his werewolf form. Brandon had looked to his father for comfort, and now his father was the one who was keeping us apart. I'd have to do something before it was too late. I'd have to convince Dr. Maddox that Brandon wasn't the danger that he thought he was, because I needed to be near Brandon— both at school and under the moon in his werewolf form.

lycan lunch

The next morning, I waited on the main steps of the school, watching for Brandon to arrive in his Jeep.

When that didn't happen, I lingered in the hallway to catch him at his locker. But when first bell rang and he still didn't show, I had no choice but to go into class. Brandon's seat remained empty. The clock above the chalkboard ticked as my mind raced. Had Dr. Maddox put Brandon on a plane to Europe? Had he taken him to a local hospital? Or was Brandon locked inside his guesthouse like he'd asked me to do once before?

"What's wrong with you today?" Ivy asked when the bell rang for lunch later that day.

"Nothing."

"I know you are worried about lunch," she said. "But I

guess you don't have to feel compelled to sit with Brandon since he's not here today."

"Yeah, you're right."

"Are you worried about coming back to our table?"

"What? Oh . . . yeah, I can't sit there with Heidi. It would be too weird."

"We've had a talk with the guys," Abby said authoritatively. "Heidi won't be sitting at our table. And if she does, we won't be sitting with her."

"Really?" I asked.

"Yes," Ivy concurred. "We told Jake and Dylan that if she does, then they can eat alone."

"You did?"

"I told them no tramps allowed!" Ivy said proudly.

"I guess it worked," Abby said as we entered the caf. "Look—the guys are all waiting for us and no sign of any cheerleaders."

My friends really did have my back.

Ivy sat by Jake, and Abby by Dylan.

I paused for a moment when I came upon my empty seat.

"We can spray it for germs," Ivy said.

Abby laughed, and I did as well. I was glad to be back to normal—or somewhat normal—and sat down in my seat.

Nash slid in next to me. He grinned a wide, toothpaste-commercial smile.

"I'm glad to have you back, Celeste," he said. "You know why I did it. Just to show you what you'd be missing. Like you've been showing me what I've been missing by being with Brandon."

"But that's not why—" I said.

"I know," he said resignedly. "But it hit home with me and I thought maybe it would with you, too. I'm trying to start over," he said. "I thought you might like this." He handed me a single rose.

Nash had never before displayed such a romantic gesture, public or private, and I wasn't sure how to handle it. It wasn't that I didn't like Nash. I did. But as a couple we were more different than alike. However, I admired him as a friend and still cared for him. And now that he was bent on changing and becoming a more mature and serious suitor, I couldn't help but feel awkward. I didn't want to reject him in front of our friends, and I really didn't want Brandon to walk in and see me holding a rose from another guy. Nash was charming and charismatic, but I couldn't help but be in love with the one guy who wasn't in the lunchroom today.

"Thank you," I said sincerely. I imagined Nash taking the time to buy it at a store on his way to school, and the flower was beautiful. It was truly sweet and thoughtful. I had to admit I was flattered that he was thinking of me in this way.

"Aw!" my friends cooed.

"That's so romantic," Abby said.

"I know. Why can't you guys be more like Nash?" Abby asked.

"He brought another girl to our table yesterday," Dylan

charged. "That's what you want?"

"That's not why she was here," Nash retorted. "Celeste knows the real reason."

"Yeah, to get back at her for sitting next to Brandon," Jake said.

"No," Nash said, still in the hot seat. "That's not why."

"Then why?" Jake asked. Nash wasn't used to talking feelings in front of our clique.

He nervously drummed his fingers on the table and fidgeted trying to come up with the right words. "I wanted her to see what life was like without me."

I was shocked. I was surprised to see Nash lay his feelings out so honestly before everyone. He was truly changing.

My friends must have been as surprised as I was. They paused for a moment, then Ivy and Abby sighed. "How romantic," they said in unison.

Dylan and Jake rolled their eyes and burst into laughter.

"Wow—you are the charmer," Dylan said, nudging his friend.

"So it was more like a prank?" Jake whispered. "To get back at her?"

"Uh . . . yes," Nash agreed, but I knew better.

"Man, you are good," Dylan said softly. "It really worked."

"Let's put the flower in a cup and we can use it as our centerpiece," Ivy suggested. Before she could take it from me, I placed it on my lap.

"I'll put it away for later," I said. I gingerly placed the rose in my backpack, out of sight.

As we started to settle in, my mind drifted away from our table, and I glanced over to Brandon's table and saw his seat still empty.

Dylan must have caught sight of me gazing toward the Westsider's table. "Finally we don't have to see you girls fussing over that weirdo," he said.

"We don't fuss over him," Ivy shot back.

"You bet you do," Dylan went on. "Since he returned your dog, it's like you've started an Eastside chapter of the Brandon Maddox Fan Club."

"Jealous?" Abby said.

"Not even close!" Dylan scowled.

"Well, now you see how he is," Jake said. "Probably so freaked out he can't come to school."

"Is that what you wanted?" I asked.

"Uh, no. But you don't want to be seen with a wolfman, do you?" Dylan snapped.

"Well, we don't want to be seen with an airhead cheerleader, either," Abby shot back.

As we began eating, I did feel a sense of relief being back with my friends. Of course, I longed to be with Brandon, but since he wasn't even here, I was glad to have Ivy's and Abby's usual lighthearted banter take my mind off of what had happened last night.

I looked again at Brandon's table, where his seat remained empty. I wondered where he might be and what he might be up to. Nash must have noticed.

"I knew it would work," Nash said so only I could hear.

"I came back because I wanted to sit with my friends," I said.

"But I am one of your friends, right?" he asked.

"Yes, you are. But . . ."

"And I've been more . . ." he hinted. "Your boyfriend, too."

"Yes. But—"

"It's still a full moon," he said. "Creatures will be out tonight. Dangerous ones."

"Keep your voice down." I tried to shush him.

"And you came back to me. You made the right choice this time. My plan worked. I knew if you saw me with someone, you'd remember what you were missing. And here you are."

"But that isn't—"

"It's what I wanted, Celeste. And I think you did, too." He reached his hand across the table and placed it over mine. Ivy and Abby caught his move and winked at me.

I couldn't help but note the irony. I'd spent nights being kissed by Nash and was often happy in his strong embrace at movies or parties. But too often, I'd felt like I wasn't important to him. I had to compete with his athletic schedule. He paid more attention to leather balls and winning scores than to me. Now that I wasn't paying him attention and was focused on Brandon, Nash seemed to see it as a challenge that he couldn't face with a team behind him. He needed to win this one on his own, and he wasn't giving up the fight. With basketball ending and baseball beginning, Nash had time to take on another sport—love. Nash appeared driven to win, and his courting me this way would have made him more attractive if I hadn't been so distracted with Brandon. Otherwise, his attention was tempting, to say the least. It was hard not to fall under his charms—I'd had feelings for him, and they hadn't gone away completely. I'd just had deeper feelings for someone else.

Before I could withdraw my hand from Nash's, Ivy snapped a picture with her cell phone.

"You guys could get Cutest Couple in Class. I'll send this off to the yearbook," she said with a smile.

Ivy was happiest when the sixsome was intact. I couldn't blame her. I wanted everyone to be happy, too, but I wasn't sure that my happiness was the same as hers.

After lunch, I headed off to the annex buildings to philosophy and I heard a whistle coming from the wooded area behind the gym. When I heard it again, I took a closer look and saw a figure standing in the brush. It was Brandon. I raced down the hill as fast as I could. I reached him to find him wearing only jeans. He appeared worn out and exhausted. He had twigs in his hair and dirt stains on his jeans and body. And though it wasn't winter, there was still a nip in the air. He was shivering.

"Take my hoodie," I said.

"No, that's okay."

I didn't listen to him. Instead, I unzipped and removed my jacket and wrapped it around his shoulders.

"Where have you been?" I asked. "I've been so worried about you."

"I didn't go home last night," he said.

"You've been out all night?"

He nodded.

"You ran away?" I asked.

"I didn't run away—I just didn't go back."

"You need to see your father. He's the only one who can help you. He's already sent in your samples. Maybe he can work on a cure."

"But—I can't let him see me like this. You saw how he acted. I shouldn't have called him."

The final bell began to ring off in the distance. "You have to go—" he said. "I have to go—"

"But where are you going?"

"I don't know. Meet me after school. I'll text you where I'll be."

He drew me into him and gave me a kiss that made me forget about classes, school, and life without my hoodie.

"You have a leaf in your hair," Abby said when I finally got to my seat in philosophy. "What gives?"

"Uh, I guess it just fell from a tree," I said. I untangled the stem from my hair and removed it.

"Where's your hoodie?" Ivy asked. "You were wearing it

at lunch. It's too cold for a T-shirt."

"Uh . . . I'm fine," I said. "Spring is almost here."

"But it's not here today," Ivy said. "I think she's just heated up from her lunch with Nash." She put her arm around me. "Right?"

"Right," I said, resigned.

"We are all going out tonight," Ivy said. "The guys are free and so are we."

"What should we do?" Abby asked. "Bowling? Indoor putt-putt?"

"The mall?" Ivy suggested.

"The guys hate the mall," Abby said.

I was distracted, thinking of the one person I wanted to be sharing the evening with.

"Let's hang out and watch movies," Ivy said.

"We've been to my house already," Abby whined. "And my mom's pissed that her snow globe was broken."

"We go to mine all the time," Ivy remarked.

"Then why don't you come to mine?" I asked, joking. I knew it was a safe invite, and maybe the whole evening would be canceled since we couldn't agree on a location.

"We never go to yours," Abby said.

"There's a reason," I replied. "I don't have a basketball court in the basement."

"Well, neither do we," Ivy challenged. "I think it's a great idea."

"You do?" I asked.

"Your house is so cozy," Ivy said.

"Yeah, and your parents are cool," Abby said.

"Uh . . . I can't," I said.

"Why?" she asked. "What are you doing?"

"I'm not sure."

I wasn't, in fact. It was a full moon, and I planned to visit Brandon. But if his father was forbidding me to see him under the moonlight, I wasn't sure how I'd get to be with him.

"We'll be at your house at seven," Abby said. "I'll bring the movies."

"And we're not inviting Brandon," Ivy said, causing my two friends to laugh.

"Uh . . . you can be sure of that," I said.

After school I waited in my car, not knowing where to go to meet Brandon. I wasn't sure if I should go home or just drive around town until he called.

I felt a wave of relief when I heard Frank Sinatra sing, "Fly Me to the Moon." I picked up my text.

Meet me in Willow Park by the lake.

Willow Park was a public forest with trails, picnic benches, and a beautiful lake. It didn't take me long to drive there. When I pulled in, I saw only a few cars parked in the lot. There weren't many people out walking this time of year and at this time of day, but in a few weeks, with the trees and flowers blooming, Willow Park would be filled with Legend's Run residents.

I walked the tree-lined path to the lake, where I found Brandon, fully clothed this time, waiting by a picnic bench.

"Are you okay?" I asked.

"Yeah. I managed to get back home."

"Did you see your father?"

He shook his head. "He thinks I'm dangerous."

"It has to be shocking for him to see you in this condition," I said. "He is your father. He loves and cares for you—"

"But I'm not what he thinks I am—I'm not dangerous."

"I know."

"I could see the fear in his eyes." Brandon looked sad. "He was terrified of me. My dad is a gentle man. I'd fight off anything that scared him. And to think the one thing he's afraid of . . . is me?"

Brandon sat on the picnic table and dropped his head in his hands in despair.

"It will be okay." I caressed his back, trying to comfort him.

"And the way he took you away from me. It broke my heart."

"Look. It's the first time he's seen you turn. It's very shocking. I was totally weirded out for a while after seeing you change. I didn't know if what I saw was real—or what to do or think."

"I can imagine . . ."

"So naturally your father is very concerned for you. And he was protective of me. I see where you get your heroism."

"He came after me with that needle."

"But he's trying to help you. You have to let him."

"I'm not afraid of needles," he said. "But under the moonlight—I wasn't going to let anyone or anything touch me."

"I'm sure that is an animal instinct," I said. "No pun intended."

"I don't know what to do, Celeste."

"I think you have to let him help you," I said gently. "What other choice do we have?"

"But how can I if he's going to keep you away from me?"

Though it pained me to say it and it meant I'd have to be away from Brandon, I told him, "Because it is for your own good."

"I need to be with you," he said. "That is my only cure."

I gave him a tight squeeze.

"It's only two more nights." I tried to assure him as much as myself. But I felt ripped apart from Brandon when we were separated for even a moment, much less two nights—especially when he was in werewolf form. There was something cosmic that drew me to him under the full moon. I wasn't sure if I could be kept apart from him, either.

"My father is all I've ever had," he said. "We don't fight—he's amazing. But now to see him fear me—I can't take it. And for him to believe I'd harm him—or you—is unbearable to me."

He rested his head on my shoulder. Brandon was exhausted from the enormous pressure he had endured the last few months. It was one thing to deal with being a transfer student in a new town, in a star-crossed love relationship, and quite another being a werewolf, too.

"So you'll let him help you?" I asked.

"How can you be so sure it will work?"

"Because it has to," I said.

"You're always so optimistic. That's one of the things I like about you. It's nice to be around positive energy, and a pretty face."

He kissed me for a long time, and we spent the next few hours cuddling together before the sun set and he had to return home to the hilltop in the woods.

TEN

wild thing

I didn't want to be apart from Brandon, but I had to keep my needs separate from his—my desire to confess to my friends that I was in love with him and my longing to be with him as a werewolf had to take a backseat to his need to be cured.

Ivy, Abby, and the gang were coming over, and I hoped it would keep my mind occupied and not focused on whatever Brandon's father needed to do to keep him safe and find an antidote. My parents agreed to go out to another movie so I could have my friends over.

I felt so awkward waiting for the gang to arrive. We didn't have a media room with a fifty-inch big-screen TV, leather theater chairs, or a popcorn machine. Instead, we'd be watching TV in our small family room. It was going to be cozy, to say the least.

Ivy and Abby arrived together with a stack of movies, and Jake, Dylan, and Nash showed up with drinks and chips.

"We weren't sure what to watch, so we brought a few choices," Abby said.

"Since it is a full moon," Ivy said cheekily, "I thought we'd watch *An American Werewolf in London*."

Jake howled, and Dylan joined him.

I loved the movie and had watched it several times on Halloweens past—but tonight it wasn't going to distract me from the day's events, just remind me of Brandon.

"You know what they say about a full moon! People act crazy," Ivy said.

"When should I start?" Jake said, making some growling noises. He nuzzled up to Ivy, sending her into giggles.

Dylan tugged Abby's belt and pulled her to him for a quick kiss. "Is that crazy enough for you?" he asked.

Nash looked to me for signs of what kind of affection to show. He wasn't about to make a move in front of everyone—as he wasn't sure how I'd respond.

We all flopped onto the couches, and Nash ended up next to me. I couldn't help but inhale his sexy body-wash scent. He scooted so close to me I thought he was going to wind up in my lap. For a moment I was lost in the world that had once been. The sixsome, together.

Champ suddenly began barking incessantly by the back door.

"What the . . . ?" Jake said, pointing to the family room window.

"What? A ghost?" Abby said.

"You have to see this," Jake said.

We all gathered around the window to find two beady eyes staring up at us.

"It's a dog," Abby said. "Calm down."

Just then the animal howled a deep howl.

"It's a wolf!" Dylan said.

Ivy and Abby screamed.

"Lock the door!" Nash said, stepping away from the window.

"It's already locked," I said.

"Make sure," he demanded.

"Turn the lights on," Ivy said. "Maybe that will scare it away."

"We are safe, guys," I said. Even though I put on a brave face, I was nervous. What was a wolf doing howling outside my window? Was this a lone, misguided wolf? Or was this one trying to signal to me that Brandon was in trouble?"

Ivy continued to scream, and Abby threw sofa pillows against the window.

"Shoo!" she said.

"Stop that," I said. "You'll break something."

"He's staring straight at you, Celeste," Ivy exclaimed.

"Maybe it's Brandon," Jake teased.

Jake and Dylan pressed their heads against the window.

Jake made faces at the wild canine while Dylan tapped the glass.

I, too, pressed my face to the glass to see if I could see more wolves or Brandon.

Just then another howl was heard from somewhere in the backyard. The wolf's ears perked up, and he barked at me a few times. Then he turned around and disappeared.

"That was creepy!" Ivy said. "I don't want to watch that movie now."

"It's gone," I said. "It's okay."

"But what if it comes back?" Ivy said.

"I don't think it will," I said.

"Yes," Dylan confirmed. "It went off into the woods. Whatever it wanted, it doesn't want it anymore."

But the fun mood was broken. "I only brought scary movies," Ivy said, soured by the unwanted visitor.

"We can't go home now," Abby said.

We sat for a while longer, but I was distracted by the wolf, and so, it seemed, were the others. The gathering was spoiled; we couldn't lose ourselves in watching a scary movie.

"Maybe we should reschedule this," I said.

"We are being rude—" Ivy said.

"No you're not," I told her. "We'll do it again at your house—in your awesome media room."

Eventually my friends agreed to end the evening early.

"We can't leave Celeste home with a wolf running around," Abby said.

"My parents will be home soon," I said. "I'll be okay. Besides, I'm safe in a house."

"Yes, I guess so," Abby said.

"There is something about you," Ivy said. "You attract wolves."

The guys got their belongings while the girls hugged me good-bye. Nash leaned in to kiss me but I stepped back awkwardly and reached for the front door instead. I did care for Nash and still thought he was attractive. I didn't wish anything but good things for him. But I didn't want to encourage him to think I felt more deeply for him than I did or was planning on a reunion. Though I still felt compassion for my first crush and former boyfriend, I didn't have the kind of feelings for him that I had for Brandon—that unbridled passion and heavenly feeling that was true love.

They all were on the lookout as they exited my house and ran safely to their cars.

As my friends drove off, Champ began to bark again by the back door.

I heard a tap at my window. I was afraid to see the wolf back again, this time all alone in my house. I gingerly pulled a curtain back and looked out into the backyard. At first I saw nothing, but then I could make out a figure standing at the trunk of a tree a few yards away.

Gray eyes gazed back, but they were at the height of someone standing on two legs.

I raced outside and plowed into Brandon's embrace.

"I'm so happy to see you," I said.

"Me too," he said. Then he hesitated. "Nash was here."

"He's just my friend."

"But he wants to get back with you. I see it all the time."

"We are just friends. That's all."

"But I want to be your friend. I want to hang out with you and your best friends. What good am I now, standing outside in the woods, hungry like a wolf?"

I held his hand and caressed it. "I want us to be together, too," I said. "Did your father see you tonight?"

"Yes. He couldn't get what he needed. I wouldn't let him. I can't help myself when I'm like this. I guess it's just animal instinct, but at the moment that he comes at me with a needle, he's not my father and I'm not his son. He's someone I don't trust and feel is going to hurt me."

"Oh . . ." I said, disappointed for him.

"But . . . I think I might be better if you are there—"

"Why?" I asked.

"There is something I see when I look into your eyes— sweetness and goodness—in whatever form I'm in. I get this overwhelming sense that you are . . ."

I waited to hear what he might say.

". . . there to help me. Not threatening, I guess. Maybe I sense love."

I beamed with pride.

"From my father I sense fear and confusion. And it only makes me angry."

"But how can I be there when your dad doesn't want me around your house—around you—on a full moon?"

"He's like me; he wants to protect you."

"I know, but I don't need protecting. I only need you."

"Will you come back with me?"

"Now?"

He nodded.

"Of course." I liked being needed by Brandon. I felt like I could somehow repay him for my fault in all of this. He had saved me and because of that suffered this lycan affliction. I'd do anything for him.

"But I have to ask you one thing: Are you afraid of me?"

"No," I reassured him. "Maybe I should be, but I'm not."

He breathed a sigh of relief. "I can't lose you. You are the only one who makes me feel sane." He leaned in and hugged me. "Remember what I said that night we kissed, under the full moon?"

I smiled widely.

"I love you, Celeste," he said again.

"I love you, too," I said. It was as natural as if I'd been saying it to him for years.

I stared up at him. I was dying for a kiss, the kind that took my breath away, made me dizzy, and felt like I was in heaven. He was magnetic, spellbinding, hypnotic. I was drawn to him like I'd never been drawn to any other guy. He stared back at me with his wolfish gray eyes. He leaned down and kissed me so intensely I thought the ground would shake under my feet. I fell into his arms.

I held him tightly under the tree in my backyard. I wasn't about to leave him again.

I couldn't abandon him. Not now. Not ever.

When the night wore on and our kisses continued, Brandon told me it was time to go.

I agreed to meet him at the hilltop behind his house, and he withdrew into the woods. I was anxious when I drove to the Westside, wondering if Dr. Maddox's plan would work. I parked by Brandon's guesthouse and raced up the hilltop before his father could spot me.

Apollo, Brandon's grandparents' husky, was barking in the main house, and I knew that the sound of my car driving in wouldn't go unnoticed.

I was trying to find Brandon on the hilltop when I heard my name being called in the woods behind me.

"Celeste," Dr. Maddox hollered. "Celeste."

The sound got closer, and Dr. Maddox reached me before I could find Brandon.

"Brandon wants you to help him," I said. "He wants you to do the tests, but I have to be with him. It's the only way he'll be able to do it."

"But that's impossible. I will have to tranquilize him first in order to take the blood samples. You see what he's like. He didn't come home last night—or today. I don't even know where he is. He could be anywhere—doing anything."

Just then Brandon emerged from the shadows.

Brandon appeared as magnificent as he had just a short time ago. His hair was fiercely wild, and his face was laced with a handsome goatee matching his dark locks. He wore a skeptical expression and a pair of jeans. His sharp fangs glowed in the moonlight.

"Brandon!" his father gasped.

Dr. Maddox moved in front of me, blocking me from view.

Brandon growled.

"It's okay—" I said. "He's not going to hurt me—or you. Brandon needs your help, Dr. Maddox, but the only way for you to get close to him with your needle is if I am here, too." I turned to Brandon. "It's okay, Brandon. You said if I was here, it will be okay."

But Brandon wasn't appeased. He shifted uneasily, backing away toward the trees.

Then I heard Dr. Meadows's words in my head—*Beware of a bite under a full moon.* Maybe this did mean me—or Brandon's father. And maybe it meant now.

Brandon must have noticed the fear in my face. His eyes softened as if he felt sad for me.

He reached out his hand. I took it and stepped toward him. I hugged him and caressed his long locks as his father quickly scrambled around the tree on the opposite side of Brandon.

While I continued to hold Brandon, his father crept up behind him and pushed the syringe into Brandon's arm in an attempt to tranquilize him.

Brandon jerked angrily, and I fell from his embrace. He yelled out a fiery howl.

I was startled. Apparently we all were.

The needle was still stuck in his arm, but the tranquilizer hadn't been injected. Brandon turned to his father with an angry stare, and Dr. Maddox, ghost white, stared back at his son. Dr. Maddox didn't say a word, the tension in the woods as thick as the brush itself.

As Brandon continued to glare at his father, I quietly rose to my feet behind him. I quickly pushed the plunger in, then grabbed the empty syringe and withdrew it from his arm in an instant.

He whipped around to me with a maddened look. I was afraid, and the needle shook in my hand. But when we locked eyes, his mood once again softened and his tense body relaxed.

Dr. Maddox took the syringe from my shaking hand and packed it away in his bag, and we watched as Brandon stormed off. We heard him shuffling through the brush, but he soon stopped.

We cautiously crept after Brandon and found him still standing, panting heavily by a tree.

"Stay back," his father said to me.

Just then Brandon's legs wavered. He stumbled as he tried to stay upright. His eyelids started to droop, and he fought to stay standing and awake.

He grabbed the tree for support but began to lose the battle. The tranquilizer had taken over, and he was clawing at the tree as he continued to stumble. He reached out to me again, but by the time I got to him, he was already lying on the ground.

"No—" his father said. "It might be a trick."

"He wouldn't do that!" I said.

I took his hand, which was limp in mine. His eyes were closed, and he lay fast asleep. Brandon was beautiful, lying there in the woods like a sleeping prince. I continued to hold his hand, and I brushed his hair away from his face and caressed his cheek. He was warm and sweaty from his battle with us and the medication.

"I need to take a blood sample now," his father said. "I'm not sure how long the tranquilizer will last."

"I'm going to stay here with him," I replied.

"I can't let you do that," he said. "It's not safe."

"It's safe now," I said, still stroking Brandon's cheek.

His father gave up fighting me and withdrew a needle from his bag. He wiped Brandon's forearm with an alcohol swab. "Wow—it's really easy to find a vein now," he said.

He quickly stuck the needle into Brandon, who didn't even flinch. Dr. Maddox placed the samples in a plastic bag and sealed them away in his medical bag.

"I'll walk you to your car," he said.

"I told you, I want to stay here with him," I countered. Brandon was so handsome lying next to me. I wanted to stay with him all night until he awoke.

"I'm going to watch him to make sure he's all right," he said. "From a distance. I don't know when he'll wake up and what mood he'll be in, but I can only imagine. There's nothing for you to do here."

I knew I wouldn't be able to convince Dr. Maddox to let me stay, and I did feel secure knowing someone, especially a scientist, would be observing him.

Dr. Maddox patted my shoulder and guided me away from the sleeping werewolf. I felt bad for Brandon that his heroism had come to this.

"He may be angry tomorrow," Dr. Maddox said when we reached my car.

"I think I will be, too," I mumbled.

willow park

Unfortunately the next day was a Saturday, so I awoke with a bit of melancholy, knowing I wouldn't see Brandon in class. I could only imagine how Brandon would be feeling today, given his struggle with us last night. I called and texted him obsessively but didn't get a response. I got dressed and hurriedly drove to his house, but it didn't appear that anyone was home. I knocked on his guesthouse door and the main house door, but no one answered. Even Apollo wasn't barking.

I wondered if his entire family had picked up and left town. Or did Brandon flee the area or not come home and they were out looking for him? I was worried. My mind was overcome with worst-case scenarios.

When I got home, "Fly Me to the Moon" began to play.

I scrambled for my cell phone.

"Brandon?" I asked, breathless. "Are you okay?"

"Celeste?" a man's voice answered.

"Dr. Maddox?"

"Yes. I wanted to call you and say thank you for your help last night. You are braver than I am."

"Uh . . . you are welcome."

"And I think the medical profession would be lucky to have you, though I'm not sure how many patients will struggle like my son did last night."

"Where is Brandon?" I asked, worried.

"He's right here."

I breathed a huge sigh of relief.

"I just wanted to talk to you first," he continued.

"I appreciate your help, Dr. Maddox, and I'm sure Brandon does, too."

I heard a pause and another voice in the background. "Celeste," Brandon said into the phone.

"Brandon, are you okay?" I asked anxiously.

"Yes," he said. "Now that I am talking to you."

I melted hearing the comfort of his sexy voice. "How are you feeling?"

"A little moody, but I know a cure for that. It's seeing you."

I smiled into the phone.

"Meet me at Willow Park tonight?" he asked softly.

"Of course!"

"We'll have a real date," he said. "This time without my father."

I hummed, sang, and whistled the whole way to the park. It was going to be a date to remember. It was the third day of the full moon. It was the last day in this cycle that Brandon would turn into werewolf form. And if we were lucky and his father could make an antidote, then this might be the last time I saw him in werewolf form forever.

That said, Dr. Meadows's words still haunted me. But if Brandon was really dangerous, wouldn't he have bitten me already? Last night, he could have bitten me or his father— and with all his anger, he still hadn't. That's not who Brandon was as a human or as a werewolf. He was kind and generous and ultimately so magnetic that the thought of being apart from him made me physically upset.

I carried a basket with a picnic dinner for us—a baguette sandwich with layers of roast beef, along with two sodas and chocolate cupcakes I'd made and topped with plastic wolves. I'd tied a pink scarf around the handle of the basket to add a little flirty romantic flare. I wanted to bring something special for my hot carnivore. I headed out early, just before sunset, so I could set the scene in the woods before he arrived.

As I drove through the twisting roads, I noticed a car following me into the parking lot. I caught sight of it in my rearview mirror. It was a familiar Beemer. Nash had followed me.

I got out of my car in a huff.

"What are you doing here?" I asked.

"I was going to ask you the same thing."

"Nash. You can't follow me everywhere."

"Celeste, I can't let you put yourself in danger."

"I'm not in danger."

"The full moon will be out soon. Please, come with me."
He grasped my arm.

"No, Nash."

"Then I'm going to have to tell Ivy and Abby—"

"*No,* Nash. I want to tell them. They are my friends. The
truth needs to come from me."

"Then you admit it. He's really a werewolf!" Nash seemed
shocked by my statement.

"No—I admit that I'm dating him. And I'm happy to
tell them." I'd been keeping Brandon's and my romantic
relationship a secret for Brandon's sake—so he wouldn't
be more tormented at school if Nash proclaimed he'd seen
the Westsider's transformation. But the part about Brandon
truly being a werewolf—I wasn't planning on telling anyone
about that.

"It is a full moon tonight and it's almost dark, Celeste,"
he said. "I'm really asking you as your friend—come back
with me."

"And I'm asking you, as your friend, to let me go."

"Celeste—we don't have to get back together—" he
said. "It's not about that anymore. It's about you. Please.

I don't want you to get hurt."

Nash was as sincere as I'd ever seen him. This was different from when he had tried to charm me to get another kiss. He was really pleading with me not to go—for my sake, not his.

"I can't just stand here and watch you walk into a darkened place to meet a werewolf," he said. "Are you insane?"

Perhaps I was, if Brandon had been like what people might expect a werewolf to be. Dr. Maddox, Dr. Meadows, and Nash were concerned for my safety. So why was I so sure Brandon would be different? Maybe I'd been so blinded by love that I couldn't see the forest through the wolves.

I paused. For a moment I really reflected. Nash was my friend, my first crush. A guy I'd known for years. He was happy and handsome and well liked. Brandon was an outsider, a guy whose father was now afraid of him, and a werewolf. It wasn't very logical, but I knew I had to follow my heart—and that would lead me into the woods.

I turned away from Nash and made my way to the end of the asphalt before he stopped me.

"You are just going to walk into this forest alone?" he asked.

I didn't reply. He already knew the answer.

He peered in my basket—noticing the contents.

"Are these the things a werewolf eats?" he asked, the sun setting behind him. "What if it's you he's planning to eat for dinner?"

A deer shot out from the woods a few yards away from us. It stopped along a wooded brush near our cars.

"See?" I said. "It's beautiful out here."

"Yes. But you should be enjoying it with me, not some circus freak."

"But you never wanted to do these things," I charged.

"I do now," Nash said sincerely. "And I want to do them with you."

He stepped in front of me, blocking me from going any farther toward the woods, and then I noticed a pair of gray eyes a few feet behind him.

I raised my hand to him. "Uh . . . you need to stay still."

Nash and I were between a wolf and his prey.

"Don't tell me how I should behave," he said angrily.

"Nash, I'm serious." I spoke softly, my voice quavering. "There is something behind you."

"Are you pranking me?"

I shook my head with fear.

"What is it?" he asked.

"A wolf," I whispered.

"Now I know you're pranking!"

He swung around so quickly that he startled the wolf. It growled low and fierce. Nash gasped and, in the motion, twisted and lost his footing. He stumbled.

The wolf must have thought Nash was attacking. The animal sprang forward and within a heartbeat had taken Nash's arm in its mouth.

Nash yelled a horrible, gut-wrenching yell.

I screamed and dropped the basket.

Nash tried to kick the wild wolf away, but it kept its jaws clamped on his arm.

I screamed again as I searched the area for a branch or anything to help.

Just then I heard another howl from the woods.

The wolf's ears perked up, and he released Nash. Nash yanked his arm away and stepped back from the wolf.

The wolf stared at Nash and growled as Brandon raced out of the woods and jumped between Nash and the wild wolf.

Brandon stared at the wolf with such fierce intensity that the wild animal retreated in fear, backing away slowly before turning and loping off into the woods.

I was very relieved but still scared, and tears streamed down my face.

"Are you okay?" Brandon asked me, resting his hands on my shoulders and looking at me squarely. His gray eyes stared down at me. I could barely nod my head.

"But he's not," I said, pointing to Nash.

Brandon noticed blood dripping from Nash's arm and ran to the basket. He untied the scarf from the wicker handle and handed it to me.

"I thought that thing was going to kill me," Nash said, in shock.

"You're all right now," I said, trembling. "It's over."

I tied my silk scarf around Nash's arm, just like I'd done to Brandon in the wintry woods. The pink scarf was quickly dotted bloodred.

Nash was clearly shaken. The things he feared most in life—wolves—had attacked him. Maybe he had a sense about them all his life. Legend's Run was known for a wolf population, but Nash wasn't a hunter, and before this school year, we hadn't seen any up close and personal. I always found his fear to be odd, but it was one of the things that made Nash vulnerable.

I rubbed Nash's back as he was, understandably, still visibly shaken.

"It's okay, man," Brandon said. "You'll be okay."

"I can't believe you look so different," Nash said. "You look like a wolf yourself."

Brandon cracked a smile, exposing two sharp lycan fangs.

"You'd better drive him to the hospital," Brandon instructed.

Brandon didn't have time to kiss me good-bye before he disappeared into the woods. His gray eyes shone through the edge of the woods as I drove Nash out of the park.

Instead of spending a romantic date with Brandon in the woods, I hung out with Nash and his family at the hospital while he got his wounded arm stitched.

Though the handsome jock might never admit it, I knew he was grateful to Brandon for saving him from the wolf.

Nash was tested for rabies, and the doctors said we would know within a few hours if he was infected. But it wasn't rabies that gave me cause for concern. I thought that Nash might be safe because he didn't have the werewolf blood that Mr. Worthington had talked about having in his own ancestry running through him.

Or did he?

catfight

I spent the next day, Sunday, inside, worried and exhausted from last night's events. Everything I was doing seemed to be bringing harm to others—Brandon saving me in the woods and now Nash following me, both resulting in them being attacked by wolves. I didn't have the strength to leave my home, and at this point I wasn't sure if I should. I used the time to regroup and hope that my lack of presence would ensure no one was harmed.

The following day at school, Nash was greeted by the student body as if he were a hero. The story that floated around the hallways, locker rooms, and classes, and took on a life of its own, was that Nash had saved me from the wolf and was bitten in the process. He held out his bandaged arm like a warrior on a battlefield.

Nash was getting the acclaim Brandon deserved. Both times. It was Brandon who'd saved me from a wolf pack when I was lost in the woods, and it was Brandon again who'd saved Nash from an attacking wolf. And somehow, Nash got the credit. But I knew it wasn't a good idea to tell anyone what really happened—especially that Brandon was a werewolf.

"Brandon saved your life," I said to Nash later that day.

"How are you so sure? Maybe he was the one who sent the wolf out there."

"How can you even think that? The wolf was stalking a deer. Brandon helped you!"

"And how can you be so naive? You saw how he was . . . he's not human."

I was fuming. I knew it was his pride that kept him from admitting the truth: that because he didn't believe me he stumbled, and the wolf, feeling threatened, attacked him.

"Are you okay?" Ivy asked Nash when she got to class. "Celeste called me from the hospital."

Nash flashed his bandaged arm like a medal.

"I can't believe you were bitten," Abby said, examining the bandage.

"Maybe it really was a werewolf," Dylan added.

"A picnic in the woods," Ivy said. "How romantic. But no wonder you came across a wolf. Haven't you ever heard of a restaurant?"

"Maybe Nash should stick to movies," Jake said.

I was about to tell my friends right there and then that it was Brandon who had saved us from the wolf when my hero entered the classroom.

Brandon locked gazes with me as he took his seat. The girls continued to coo over Nash's wound as Nash turned back to Brandon and gave him a thankful nod.

After class, Brandon gestured for me to meet him. I gathered my books and told my friends I'd catch up to them and found him waiting for me underneath the staircase.

"My dad left today for Europe," he said. "He's going to try to make an antidote."

"That's great news!" I said, giving him a hug. "How long do you think it will take?"

"It will take a while, but he said he'd check on me and let me know as soon as he has something."

"That's terrific!" I said. I snuggled up to Brandon. I imagined what our life would be like together without the threat of his transformations.

"I was going to tell my friends about you saving Nash," I said. "They don't have to know why or how you saved him, only that you did."

"It's over with now. I'm just glad you're okay—and that he is, too."

Brandon's caring nature made my love for him even deeper. It was then I knew I couldn't keep the secret any longer.

***

I found Ivy and Abby at a round table in the library. Ivy was fiddling with her makeup, and Abby was working on homework.

I didn't plan on telling them every detail about Brandon and me, but I was bursting to tell them it was him who I was interested in—not Nash. How could I continue to keep this a secret when my heart was going to explode with love every time I saw or even thought of him? And to see Nash parade himself around school as a self-proclaimed hero when in fact he'd have been torn to shreds if it hadn't been for Brandon? I was sure Nash wouldn't tell them that it was a werewolf that saved him, but I knew that my former boyfriend wasn't in the position to publicly disparage Brandon now. There were two witnesses Saturday night who knew who'd really saved him from the attacking wolf. And Nash had more to lose by us telling everyone he wasn't the hero than Brandon had in Nash proclaiming the Westsider was a werewolf. It was time to come clean. I sat down and was anxiously bouncing in my chair when Abby looked up from her textbook.

"Stop shaking the table," she said. "You're making me seasick."

"I have something to tell you," I said intently.

"Wow, Celeste," Abby said, "you look like you have major news."

"Are you and Nash engaged?" Ivy teased, putting her compact in her purse.

"It's about Brandon," I said.

"Brandon?" Abby asked.

"You want us to invite him somewhere else again?" Ivy asked. "I think we've done enough babysitting. Besides, Jake is getting really freaked out that we've been including him. I think he gets jealous. I mean, he has nothing to worry about, though—as if!"

Ivy was making this difficult confession even more challenging. "No," I said. "It's not that."

"Then what?" Abby asked.

"I have a confession."

"Oh . . ." Abby said. "Sounds serious. What is it?"

"Did you paint Brandon's Jeep?" Ivy asked.

"No!" I said.

"Then what is it?" she said, waiting for details.

"I like . . . uh . . . I . . ."

"Just spill it out!" Ivy ordered.

"I like Brandon!" I exclaimed. There it was. I'd laid out my confession to my friends. It was like a huge weight off of me. I only had to wait now for their response.

"Brandon?" Ivy asked, shocked.

"Duh," Abby said.

Ivy and I were surprised by Abby's response.

"What?" we both said.

"You talk about him all the time," Abby said. "Trying to invite him everywhere we go."

"So you knew?" I asked.

"This is the secret Dr. Meadows told me a friend would be keeping from me!" Ivy screeched. "I can't believe you told Abby first!"

"She didn't," Abby said in a huff. "It was intuition—I just knew."

"I haven't told anyone," I proclaimed.

"It's okay," Ivy said, resigned. "We all get crushes on people. And I guess I can see why you'd feel sympathy for your pet project. It's only natural. I think you've got that Stockholm syndrome thing."

"It's more than that," I said. "I've been seeing him."

Both girls gasped.

"What?" Ivy said. "What do you mean? You've—"

"Kissed Brandon Maddox?" Abby asked.

"Girls, keep it down over there—" the librarian admonished us.

I nodded.

"I don't believe you," Ivy said.

"I do," Abby said. "He's hot—except for being a Westsider and all."

Abby smiled. There was a tiny rebellious streak that ran through her and, though she'd never be seen dating a Westsider, my news was wildly thrilling to her.

"I can't believe this," Ivy said, trying to process the information. "But I'm glad you told us right away. We can help you now."

"So when did this happen?" Abby asked.

"Uh . . . a few months ago," I said, baring my soul.

"A few months ago?" Ivy asked, shocked again.

I nodded.

"And you didn't tell me—your best friend since first grade?" she asked.

"I'm her best friend, too!" Abby said.

"I can't believe you!" Ivy said. "You've been secretly dating Brandon Maddox and you didn't tell your own best friend?"

"Best friends," Abby reiterated.

"I wanted to—in fact I even tried."

Abby had a hard time controlling her smile.

"I guess you don't think that much of me, do you?" Ivy asked with disappointment in her voice. "All this time, not saying a word. You obviously don't think anything of our friendship—or me."

Ivy was mad—or, rather, disappointed.

"But you always teased him." I defended myself. "How could I?"

"I don't know. . . . But you should have." Ivy gathered her purse and backpack. "I don't care that he's a Westsider, Celeste. I've only wanted what was best for you. So maybe I was wrong. But at least I was honest with you, something you obviously didn't feel you could be with me."

"It didn't happen like that, Ivy. Let me explain."

Ivy turned her nose up and stood.

"What are you doing?" Abby asked.

"I can't sit here anymore. Not with her."

"Ivy," I said, "let's talk—please."

But Ivy was inconsolable. I knew enough about her to know she'd need to cool off. But I'd never been the object of her disappointment, and it broke my heart that I now was. If I had it to do over, I would have loved to have told her sooner. But it was her repulsion toward the Westsiders that made it so hard to do. And whenever I'd tried, for some reason I had failed. And with Nash adding his threat to the mix, it had been put off even longer. My stomach was in knots. My best friend since first grade moved over to the other side of the room to be away from me.

But, oddly enough, Abby stayed with me.

"She'll get over it," she said.

"Will she?" I asked.

"I've been keeping a secret as well. Just like Dr. Meadows said I would."

"You're going out with a Westsider, too?" I tried to make myself laugh.

"No!" Abby said. "And Ivy will be mad with this one as well."

"What is it?" I asked.

"Since you've confessed," she said, "I'll confess, too." She paused. "But you may be really mad."

"Maybe you shouldn't tell me. I feel upset enough for one day."

"But I want to tell you. Promise you won't be mad?"

"Uh . . . sure."

Abby took a deep breath. "I know who painted Brandon's Jeep and locker."

"Nash?"

She shook her head, then leaned into me and whispered. "Jake and Dylan."

"What?" I exclaimed.

"I found out a while ago when I saw some paint in Dylan's car. He promised not to do it again."

"Why did they do that?"

"To get back at Ivy and me. They were jealous of Brandon. Silly, huh?"

"Why would they be jealous of Brandon?"

"I guess Dylan felt threatened after Brandon returned Pumpkin. I hugged Brandon in the middle of class, remember? I invited him to my party. Ivy picked him up. It didn't go over very well. Even Ivy just told you she could tell Jake was jealous."

"Wow—I never would have thought it was them."

"Are you mad that I didn't tell you?"

"No, I understand."

"I kind of thought you would—but Ivy, she's going to be livid."

"Yes, I guess she will."

"And are you mad at Jake and Dylan? Please don't be. They were doing it because of us—more so than because of Brandon."

"No," I said, my spirit still low from Ivy's anger. "It wasn't nice, but they did use water-based paints."

"I am so relieved now that I've told you."

"Me too," I said truthfully, even though I felt low.

"That's what friends are for," Abby said.

"Yes, we should have done this a while ago," I said, breaking a smile.

While Abby tied her hair into a ponytail, I pondered my future with my first best friend.

"Do you think Ivy will ever forgive me?" I asked.

"Perhaps after she forgives me," Abby said.

I gazed at my best friend, who had her back to me, while Abby was still focused on me.

"You have to tell me everything," she said. "Where, when, and why? And is Brandon a good kisser?"

I couldn't help but grin and nodded enthusiastically.

"And most important," she asked, "what are you going to do now?"

Ivy continued to ignore me for the rest of the day. She talked to Abby but shunned me, sat on the opposite end of our lunch table, and didn't wait for me after any of our classes. I was truly relieved my friends knew about Brandon but upset that Ivy was so angry with me. However, I understood her feelings. And I think she was right to feel them.

"I told Ivy and Abby," I said to Brandon after school.

"That I'm a werewolf?" he asked, surprised.

"No, silly. About us."

"What?" he asked, confused. "But I thought we were going to wait until I got a cure."

"I know. But Nash can't say anything now. He owes you his life. And he knows we could tell everyone he wasn't the one who drove the wolf away."

"Wow . . ." he said, the news finally soaking in. "So you told Ivy and Abby about us?" he asked, flattered. "How did they take it?

"Ivy hates me, and Abby admires me."

"Well—I'm sorry about Ivy . . . but Abby?"

"She thinks it's cool that—in her mind—I'm rebellious. But I'm not being rebellious. I just want to be with you."

He gave me a squeeze.

"Well, that's a shame about Ivy," he said. "I'm sure she'll come around. I guess she really detests Westsiders."

"No—it's me. She's upset I didn't think enough of her to share the truth with her right away. I do understand her feelings. And I wanted to tell her sooner—but this town is so divided, and she has always claimed to hate the Westside. I didn't want her to be mad, and I wound up making her upset anyway."

"It's okay, all of your intentions were good."

"I really am sad she's so upset with me."

"Maybe it's best if you eat lunch with her for a while longer."

"What? I thought you'd want us to start doing things together in public."

"It can wait. Don't get me wrong—I'm dying to be with you. But Ivy's been your best friend since you were kids. It's better to show allegiance to her than a guy you just met this year."

"Are you sure?"

"Yes. I can wait. But she better get over it soon!" he said.

Brandon not only was a great boyfriend but a great friend, too.

For the rest of the day and evening my calls and texts to Ivy remained unanswered. I was wondering when Abby would tell her secret to Ivy, too, and be in the doghouse with me.

something blue

The following morning, Nash stumbled into class. His hair wasn't gelled and meticulously unkempt but rather tousled as if he'd just crawled out of bed. His eyelids were droopy and his preppy clothes were wrinkled, with half of his polo collar sticking up. He carried his books like they were a football.

A few of the girls snickered at his appearance.

"Had a late night with Celeste?" Dylan asked.

Nash high-fived him. But we girls knew differently.

Abby winked at me while Ivy didn't even turn around.

The next several days, Nash continued to arrive late for class, and Ivy continued to ignore my pleas for forgiveness.

"I'm benched for a few baseball practices until this thing

heals," Nash said, looking bummed at lunch.

Ivy still sat on the opposite end of the table from me. The tension was as thick as the meat loaf the cafeteria served.

Her scorn didn't go unnoticed by the guys at the table.

"You barely even look at Celeste," Dylan said. "Catfight?"

"You can ask her," Ivy said.

"Nothing wrong over here," I said.

"She would think that," I heard her mumble.

"We are one big, happy family," Abby said to Dylan.

Abby was stuck in the middle of our feud and was doing her best not to draw attention to it.

But I was dying inside. My best friend was now acting as if I were her enemy—and maybe to her I was. It turned me inside out and made me upset to be ignored—especially by my own best friend.

I decided to do something about it, sooner rather than later.

"I want to make a peace offering to Ivy," I said to Abby later that day.

"Are you sure?" she asked. Abby hadn't told Ivy her secret; if Ivy and I reconciled, then she'd be the odd girl out once she revealed hers.

"I can't take her ignoring me any longer."

"What do you want to do?"

"Go back to Dr. Meadows's shop."

Abby perked up. "For another fortune?"

"No, I want to avoid that at all costs."

"Then what for?"

"Something blue."

Abby and I entered Penny for Your Thoughts, and I rushed over to one of the jewelry tables with bated breath, hoping the earrings were still there. I spun the rack of earrings around when I saw the blue crystals glistening back at me.

"Can I be mad at you, too?" Abby asked as I held up the sparkling jewelry in the light.

The earrings were way more than I'd ever spent on jewelry for myself or my friends. I was known more to make earrings or buy them at mall boutiques. But these were real rocks, not plastic, and cost the amount of two trips to the movies including a tub of popcorn. But today I was going to splurge for the girl who had always saved a seat on the bus for me for the past eleven years.

I was nervous about seeing Dr. Meadows, however.

"Hello, ladies . . ." she said as she greeted us at the counter. "Where is your friend?"

"Ivy?" Abby said. "We are here for a surprise. But you probably already knew," she said with a giggle.

I didn't want to give any information to Dr. Meadows— my plan was to get in the shop, pay, and get out without so much as a future warning about moons.

But Abby was all about telling Dr. Meadows our story, like she was a therapist instead of a psychic.

"Yes. She's a bit mad, and Celeste thought it would be

awesome to give her a 'forgive me' gift."

"Uh . . . yes," I politely agreed. "Ivy really liked these earrings last time we were here."

"Well, that is a good friend," Dr. Meadows said, "to think that much of her to remember what she liked and buy them for her. I can't imagine why she'd be mad at you."

"She's mad because Celeste was going out with this guy and she didn't tell her."

Abby couldn't stop talking to Dr. Meadows.

I rolled my eyes. I felt like I was with my mother when she'd blab my bra size to the saleswoman even though I could look in the bin myself. Too much information.

"Ahh . . . you have a boyfriend?"

I shrugged my shoulders.

"But I think I already knew that," she said.

"You did?" Abby said, surprised. "Celeste told you? Ah . . . of course you knew. You read her mind."

But in fact I was the one who had told Dr. Meadows that I had feelings for a guy who I thought was changing into a werewolf.

"I'd just like to buy these, please," I said, trying to change the subject.

"So who is this mystery man?" Dr. Meadows pried. She knew whoever he was must be the guy that I thought was a werewolf but refused to reveal to her.

I wasn't about to tell her. Not now or ever.

"It's Brandon Maddox!" Abby blurted out. "Do you

know him? He lives around here."

My mouth dropped wide open. I was shocked and horrified by Abby's blabbing. I didn't even have the chance to hush, nudge, or quiet her before his name and location were handed to the one woman I didn't want to have the information.

"No, I don't think I know him," Dr. Meadows said.

I was only slightly relieved, because as long as she knew his name, she could search him out.

"Is he related to Sophie and Franklin Maddox?" Dr. Meadows suddenly asked.

Those were Brandon's grandparents, but I wasn't about to give her any more information.

"I think it's time we go," I said. "Abby is almost late for volleyball practice."

"Oh, yes," Abby said, realizing the time.

I handed Dr. Meadows my money, and she placed the earrings in a box.

"Would you like me to wrap this?" she asked.

"No, thank you," I said hurriedly. "I can do that at home."

"Please come again, girls, and bring Ivy with you. I know she'll cool off after she sees what she means to you."

That was one prediction she'd made that I hoped would come true.

"Okay!" we both said as we headed for the door.

"Oh, and Celeste," she called after me. "Be sure to bring Brandon, too."

I scowled inside but smiled sweetly on the outside. Before she could come from behind the counter and attempt to give me another of her unwanted psychic predictions, I raced out of the shop and into the safety of my car.

The next morning, I unlocked Ivy's locker. We all knew one another's combos as if they were our own. The inside of her locker was decorated with pictures of our sixsome together.

I placed the package I'd wrapped with pink paper and a whimsical purple bow on the top shelf, along with a card I'd made for her.

I waited at the end of the hallway with a watchful gaze. When she arrived at her locker and opened it, she picked up the gift.

"It's from Celeste," she whispered. She must have recognized my handwriting.

Abby nodded. "You should open it."

"Of course I'm going to open it. It's a present. Hey, maybe this is that unexpected gift Dr. Meadows told me about!"

Ivy opened the card and read my touching note. "Aww . . ." she said.

Then she unwrapped the gift.

"She bought me the earrings I loved!" she said. "That was so nice of her!"

I headed over to her locker as she caught sight of me.

"I'm sorry—" I began.

"Me too!" She opened her arms for a best friends embrace. "I missed you!"

"Me too!"

We squeezed each other so hard I knew that she, too, had really missed me during the days we'd spent apart.

"I love these earrings," she said. She quickly took off the gazillion-dollar ones she was wearing and replaced them with the ones I'd bought for her.

"I'm so glad you do," I said, relieved we were back to normal. The blue crystals shined brightly against her lustrous blond hair.

"I wanted to tell you," I said.

"I shouldn't have made fun of him," she apologized.

Abby stood with her arms folded as Ivy and I ended our feud.

I was so happy to have my friend back, I almost teared up.

We headed into class and chatted like we'd been doing every day since elementary school until the ringing bell ceased our gossip session.

a new nightmare

Before I got to the cafeteria, Nash pulled me aside. "I have to talk to you about something."

"Are you going to tell me who painted Brandon's Jeep?" I asked. "Because I already know."

My former boyfriend paused for a moment with a quizzical look. "No, that's not it. I really need to talk to you."

"All right," I said. He led me into the empty speech and drama classroom. A rack of clothes and boxes of shoes and accessories were stacked at the back of the room. Nash and I sat in chairs face-to-face, so closely our knees were touching.

"So what's going on?" I asked.

"I can't sleep," he whispered.

"I know—you haven't really been yourself lately. But I've had a lot on my mind with my fight with Ivy—so I'm sorry I didn't ask you about it earlier. How's your arm?"

"I think I'm going to have a scar for sure. But the problem is I've been having trouble sleeping. I think I'm having post-traumatic stress or something."

"I'm sure you are. It's understandable."

"So you think that's it?"

"Yes. It was traumatic. It was awful for me just seeing you being attacked," I said truthfully. "I'm sure for you it was horrendous."

"I just can't shake that night," he said with a far-off look. "Ever since, I've felt really odd."

Odd? That didn't sound good. "What do you mean?"

From his furrowed expression, I could tell he was worried. "I have these bizarre dreams, and I wake up really exhausted."

Dreams? "Maybe it's the medications for your bite."

"You think so?" he asked as if he hadn't thought of that himself. "I hope so."

"Maybe you should see the school nurse," I offered.

"She'll send me to a shrink."

"Why would she send you to a shrink over dreams? We all have wild dreams."

He placed his hand on top of mine. "I dream about that night," he said.

I didn't want to hear any more. "You've always had a fear of wolves," I consoled him. "It's only natural to—"

But he didn't take his hand away. "I know if I tell you—you

won't say anything to Ivy or Abby."

"Of course not, but you don't have to tell me. I don't think I really want to know."

His grasped my hand intently. "I dream I'm a wolf," he said.

My heart plummeted to the pit of my stomach. *Oh no,* I thought. *Not again. Not Nash!*

"Isn't that weird?" he asked, a bit shaken. "Odd? Bizarre?"

"It's probably just nerves," I said, trying to reassure him as much as I was trying to reassure myself. I wasn't about to accept the alternative—that Nash could be experiencing what Brandon had before he turned into a . . .

"But to be safe, why don't we go to the nurse?" I said.

Nash took both of my hands in his. They were strong and a little rugged from playing sports. "This feels like before," he said, "when we were dating. I'm not sure why I always messed it up with you. I know it sounds cliché . . . but you are the best thing that ever happened to me."

His words were so honest and caring that it really did shake me inside.

I laughed nervously. I didn't know what to say. These were the best moments, when Nash's armor was removed and I could see deep down in his soul. I always sensed that he didn't share his truest thoughts or emotions with other girls—that, for some reason, he only shared his fears and dreams with me. It was something I wished he would have confessed and realized when we were dating.

But now wasn't the time to consider his romantic feelings for me. I had to get him to the nurse to see if his dreams and strange feelings might just be the result of an infection from the wolf bite.

The nurse didn't find anything out of the ordinary with Nash and sent him back to class. I was relieved, but only slightly.

After school, when Brandon and I were alone on the hilltop, I shared Nash's confession with him. "Nash told me he's been having strange dreams."

"About you? I see how he is trying to make his comeback with you."

"No, it's worse than that."

"What could be worse than that?"

"He dreams he's a wolf."

"You don't think . . ." Brandon looked concerned.

"It's not possible. You are related to the Legend's Run werewolf, Nash isn't."

"Then I'm sure it's nothing. Just bad dreams."

"That would be awesome," I said. "But I just wanted you to know."

"I'm glad you told me. There's something I want you to know, too."

"What?"

"I got word from my dad today," Brandon said enthusiastically. "He told me he's getting close to an antidote."

"You're kidding!" I exclaimed.

"Wouldn't it be great if he had something for me before the next full moon?"

I rested my head against his chest.

"It's funny," he said. "I think I might miss it. There is some part of me that seems to crave those nights."

"I guess it's in your blood."

"And the way you look under the full moonlight. It's extraordinary."

"Well, if you don't mind my saying, I think I'd miss it, too."

He leaned in and kissed me. There was a tiny part of me that hoped Dr. Maddox took his time with the cure.

Brandon and I took our school relationship slowly. Though Ivy and Abby knew about Brandon, we were still concerned not to go public until his condition was cured. The vandalism stopped, but the teasing didn't. We heard "Wolfie," "Wolfman," and "Werewolf" muttered under Eastside students' breath as we walked down the halls, and I didn't want it to become worse if they found out the truth. I wasn't so worried that Nash might reveal the secret, since he seemed to be preoccupied and recovering from his own trauma regarding the attack. However, I didn't want to make life even worse for Brandon. An Eastsider dating a Westsider would be major news in our school, and though I didn't want to hide it anymore, I knew for Brandon's sake that we had to wait for the cure.

Nash continued to show up to class restless and irritable. But as the days wore on, he became increasingly interested in me. Even when I told him I only wanted his friendship, he didn't waver in his attention. Nash didn't use the threat of revealing Brandon's secret as an attempt to win me back, but rather this time he tried chivalrous and charismatic actions. He was more charming to me than he ever had been. And though Nash opened doors for me, texted and called me, and mostly ignored every other girl who came his way, it didn't change my feelings. I had one heart, and it was meant for Brandon.

FIFTEEN

the cure

Moonlight Dance flyers and signs were posted all around the school. The annual dance welcomed in the beginning of spring and was an event every student hoped to attend.

I was eyeing a poster while I was waiting to meet Ivy and Abby after class and dreaming of what it would be like to be Brandon's date. He'd wear a stunning sport coat, and I'd wear a tea-length dress that shimmered like diamonds. Everyone would watch us dance together as the moonlight shined above.

Then I realized—the moonlight. I pulled out my calendar and frantically flipped through the pages. And there it was— staring at me in the face—FULL MOON. Brandon would be a werewolf that night. My heart plummeted to my shoes.

Suddenly someone tweaked my sides and I screamed.

"You are so easily spooked!" Nash said.

"Uh . . . I was just . . ."

"Thinking about the dance?"

"Uh . . . I guess."

"I was, too. And I wanted to know if you'd be my date."

I was shocked. I certainly didn't think he'd ask me, knowing I had feelings for Brandon. And I assumed he would be taking Heidi Rosen.

"I figured you wouldn't be going with you-know-who," he said, "being that it will be a full moon and all. Do you already have a date?"

Nash had me trapped. Brandon hadn't even asked me yet. I didn't know what to say. "Well . . . uh . . . no," I said truthfully. "But—"

"Great, then you'll go with me," he said triumphantly.

Before I could stop him, Nash kissed me on the cheek and said, "I'll get tickets," and took off down the hall.

I was left standing there, dumbfounded, when Ivy and Abby arrived.

"Well, then everything will be back to normal," Ivy said when I told her what happened.

Even though we were fine, she still longed for us to remain a sixsome—the original sixsome.

"I'm not so sure. I really wanted to go with Brandon." I was relieved I no longer had to hide my affection for the Westsider from my friends and was happy to admit the truth to them, even if I'd gotten myself in a jam.

"Did Brandon ask you?" Abby wondered excitedly.

"No," I said. "The signs were just posted. It's his first year here—so he wouldn't even know about the dance."

"Well, it seems to me that you're in quite a pickle!" Abby said.

Brandon caught up to me after fifth bell. He seemed really excited about something. "I wanted to talk to you," he said brightly. "Do you have a minute?"

"Yes." I couldn't think of anything I'd rather be doing than be with Brandon, and anything could be put off till later to make that happen.

We stepped into an empty alcove next to the library.

"I saw the signs about a Moonlight Dance coming up," he said.

"Oh?" I said.

"I wanted to check with you—before anyone else had a chance to ask you. You can say no—since I'm a Westsider and all," he said with a cute smile, "but would you want to go to the Moonlight Dance with me?"

"I'd love to!" I blurted out.

"Great!" he said.

"But there's one problem," we both said in unison.

We both laughed.

"You first," he said. Brandon gazed down at me lovingly.

"No, you," I said.

"It will be a full moon—" he began.

"I know."

"But . . . I'm hoping my dad will have sent me the antidote by then. And we'll be good to go."

"Oh . . . okay."

"Now what is your problem?" he asked me.

"Uh . . ." I couldn't bring myself to tell him about the Nash situation.

"It's okay, you can tell me."

"I don't have anything to wear!"

After school, Ivy, Abby, and I went to the mall in search of dresses for the Moonlight Dance. My friends were thrilled to have any excuse to shop.

"So, Celeste, you can buy one dress to wear for Nash and one to wear for Brandon," Abby teased.

"Maybe you should pick Nash," Ivy said. "Maybe it will rekindle your feelings for him again."

Abby and Ivy found tons of dresses to try on while I still sifted through the racks trying to find one that I thought might look all right.

"At least pick something," Ivy said.

I saw a teal blue dress with a thin black belt. It was gorgeous. Then I noticed the price. My heart almost burst through my chest.

"I can wear one of Juliette's," I said.

"Whatever!" Ivy took the dress from my hand and

somehow managed to drape it over her other ones and tee-tered her way to the dressing room.

I reluctantly followed behind.

Abby modeled a lavender strapless while Ivy posed in a blue dress. I could see my two friends looked amazing as I peered from my dressing-room door.

"Come on over here!" Abby said.

I tiptoed out in my bare feet.

"You look gorgeous!" Abby shouted.

"You have to buy it!" Ivy cheered.

"So, you'll wear this with Nash," Ivy said.

"I think it will match Brandon's eyes," Abby said.

I imagined my old self, happy that Nash was paying me so much attention and generously making all efforts to be there for me. And I imagined my new self with Brandon, happier than I'd ever been—but torn for the guy who had to hide from a full moon.

The one thing I couldn't have imagined was the predicament I was in now. Movie or TV stars might have these problems, but not someone like me.

It was a week before the dance and Nash appeared to be feeling great. His bandage and stitches were removed and he was able to play baseball. He showed off his scar, while Brandon continued to hide his under his fingerless gloves. I was relieved that my former boyfriend seemed not only back to normal but was more enthusiastic and happy than I'd seen him in months. I tried to tell him about Brandon and the dance, but every time I broached the subject, he either dismissed it or changed the topic. I wasn't sure if maybe he already knew and was just trying to avoid the situation.

Nash was my friend—and my first boyfriend—and I wasn't the type to feel good when hurting others. I wanted to proceed with caution in telling him. Nash was more focused on me than when we dated. He made a point to ignore Heidi Rosen and was attentive toward me. I had to wait for the right moment to convince him I would be attending the dance with Brandon.

"You have to come over," Brandon said one day after school.

His tone was urgent and emphatic. I was nervous about what could be so important that Brandon would have me come over immediately.

When I arrived at his guesthouse, Brandon didn't even kiss me, but instead, enthusiastically led me to his desk. An open shipping box was sitting on it, with brown mailing paper lying next to it. The postmark was from Geneva.

"Here it is," he said.

"What is it?"

"The antidote." He led me over to the desk.

"You're kidding!"

"No," he said, pleased.

"What do you do with it?" I asked. I didn't touch the small, oil-filled vial but rather examined it from a safe distance.

He took it out of the box. "I drink it."

"It doesn't look like it would taste very good."

"I guess not," he said with a laugh.

"So, when do you take it?"

"Just as the sun sets on the next full moon," he said, placing it back in the box.

"This is great news!"

"Yes. Then we can go to the dance the following night."

"And we can date at school!"

We embraced. He picked me up and swung me around.

"So how did Nash react when you told him you were going with me?"

"Uh . . ." I said as I got my bearings.

"You haven't told him yet?" he asked.

"I've been trying to—"

"You have to tell him," he said.

"I know," I said, ashamed of myself.

"Do you want me to tell him?" he asked, towering over me.

"I'm not sure that's the best idea."

"I figured not," he said with a clever grin.

He took my hand and led me back to the vial.

"There is one issue, however. My dad says the antidote hasn't been tested on humans. Well . . . for obvious reasons. He doesn't know any other werewolves."

"I guess not."

"Since it hasn't been tested, he says there is a small

chance . . . that it will have the opposite outcome."

"I'm not sure what you mean."

"There is a small chance that it can make me a werewolf full-time."

"That's a huge risk!" I said.

"I wanted you to know."

"So you could be a werewolf under any moon?"

"Yes," he answered.

"What will you do?" I asked.

"I don't know. What would you do?"

I wondered what I'd do. Of course, I wouldn't want to be a werewolf even three times a month—so I surely wouldn't want to be one every night. But Brandon? I wasn't sure what to tell him I'd do.

"I don't know. . . ." I said. "I really don't know."

"On the one hand, there's the chance I can be normal," he pondered. "And we could be together. On the other, I could never be normal and we could . . ."

I gazed at him. *Never have a future together?* I thought. "It is a decision you have to make, Brandon," I said, hugging him and trying to comprehend the magnitude of the situation. "I'll support you either way."

The following morning at school, I approached Nash. I knew he was going to be hurt and upset when I told him I wouldn't be able to go with him to the Moonlight Dance—and instead would be showing up with Brandon. But I had to tell him and this time let nothing get in my way.

"I need to talk to you," I said, finding him as he headed toward baseball practice.

"Me too," he said. He shot me a sexy stare and leaned on his bat. "I heard you got your dress with Ivy and Abby."

"They told you?" I asked. I assumed my friends wouldn't blab the information about their dresses to the guys—but mine? This was going to be even harder than I thought.

"Uh-huh. I know you are going to look gorgeous."

"Well . . . I have to tell you something about the dance."

"It's weird," he interrupted, "but since I got that bite, I feel so different. I feel more alive. Things taste better, I can see better. I have more energy—and I had enough before. It's like I see the world differently. Fresh. New. Maybe it's one of those near-death experiences."

"Well, I'm not sure how you are going to see this."

"What?"

"I've been trying to tell you about the dance. When you asked me . . . I didn't have the chance to tell you because you ran off so quickly."

His jovial mood quickly changed. "You're going with Brandon," he said suddenly.

I was surprised he knew. "Did Ivy and Abby tell you?"

"They didn't have to. I can see it in your face."

"I've been trying to tell you, Nash, honestly. But it seemed like you didn't want to listen to me."

"So you are ditching me for him?"

"I never said 'yes.' You ran off, and it became a misunderstanding. I've been trying to tell you ever since."

Nash tapped the top of his bat, frustrated. "He's going to be a werewolf this weekend. Not only are you going to show up with a Westsider—but a werewolf?"

"Shh," I said. "He's not going to be one. His father sent him a cure."

"A cure?" he said. "Are you crazy? He can't be cured. I saw him—he's a circus freak!"

"He is not," I argued. "He's a really kind person. He saved you, don't you remember?"

Nash turned red and got in my face. "Be my guest, Celeste. You could go with me, your first boyfriend, who is one of the most popular guys in this school." Then he looked at me intently. "A guy who is in love with you."

I was surprised by Nash's confession and left speechless. His words were kind but ultimately too late. When I didn't respond, his mood suddenly changed. "Or you could show up with a two-bit loner hick who's a werewolf."

I was shocked by his sudden outburst. I figured Nash would be angry, but I wasn't prepared for him to spew such venom.

"In fact, I'd rather not go with you," he said indignantly. "If that's your taste in men? I wouldn't want you liking me."

He placed his bat over his shoulder, turned, and walked away.

I was stunned. I knew he'd be mad, but I didn't know he'd be cruel.

As I watched my former boyfriend storm off to the field, I thought about what he'd just said. In the mix of his hatred, he had told me that he loved me. After all this time of dating him, Nash Hamilton was finally in love with me. And now I was in love with a werewolf.

SIXTEEN

in the company of wolves

I was on my way to meet Brandon at Willow Park. Brandon planned to take the antidote just before sunset, and he
wanted to celebrate with a date by the lake. I tried to convince
him he might need time to recover from the serum, but he
insisted he wanted to meet me by the shimmering water with
a full moon glowing and him being his normal human self.

As I sat on the bench and watched the sun set, I imagined
how nervous he must be, taking the serum by himself and
not knowing if his body would respond well or if it would
cause him a permanent lycan condition.

I was camped out by the lake when I felt the prickly sen-
sation of being watched. I looked around and saw a figure
standing a few yards away from me in the woods.

It probably wasn't the best idea to be waiting alone in the

park, but since it was warmer, there were more people milling about. Then I noticed that most were heading home for dinner.

"Brandon?" I asked.

But no one responded.

I thought it might be best to get to my car, so I quickly rose when the figure stepped out of the brush.

I was surprised when I saw it was Nash approaching me from the woods.

"What are you doing here?" I asked.

"I wanted to see you." Nash was sincere, but now wasn't the time for a long talk. Brandon would be here soon.

"How did you know I was here?" I asked.

"Ivy told me. I felt weird all day. I wanted you to know. I'm sorry for the way I've been acting."

"You don't have to apologize," I said. "I understand. I would be mad, too."

But Nash was as candid and gentle as I'd ever seen him.

"I said some awful things. I wanted to tell you that."

The sun was setting behind him. The sky was beautiful, with different shades of pink and purple.

"It's okay," I said.

"No. Brandon saved me that night—and I was really mean."

"But you did say one nice thing," I said.

"Yes, I did," he said with a glint in his eye. "I guess I just said it too late."

We stood awkwardly, not knowing what to say next.

As the darkness fell and the full moonlight began to glow, I stared up at my former boyfriend as he gazed down at me. He smiled a sweet smile. Then suddenly his bright expression turned sour.

"Are you okay?" I asked.

Nash's face looked strained, and then suddenly he fell to his knees.

"Nash!" I exclaimed.

He grabbed his stomach as if he was in severe pain.

"What's wrong? Are you all right?"

He gripped the grass like he was holding on for his life. He arched his back and then leaned back on his knees. He pulled his shirt off over his head.

"I'm freaking hot!" he shouted.

"Oh no!" I said.

Nash jumped up and kicked off his sneakers and pulled off his tube socks.

"No, Nash! No!" I yelled as I watched in horror.

Nash was standing in his cargo shorts. He breathed deeply and when he exhaled, out came mist like it was wintertime— only the air outside was at least sixty degrees.

"Nash—" I said. "This can't be happening!"

"What is wrong with me?" he said. "I'm burning up!"

"It might just be a fever." I tried to reassure him and myself.

I was afraid of what was happening to him. It couldn't be.

Not two guys in Legend's Run. This had to be something different. He had to just be having a spring fever. Or so I hoped.

Then Nash's eyes turned a piercing blue gray, and I knew it was worse than spring fever. He stumbled into the woods.

"Nash—" I called. "Nash."

I couldn't find him. The brush was thick, and with new leaves and buds sprouting, it was hard to see.

I heard Nash yell.

"Nash," I called back. "I'll get help!"

Then I heard a maddening howl.

I was so frightened. I covered my ears.

"Not again!" I yelled to the moon.

Nash stepped out from behind a tree. His eyes were a sharp blue gray, and his sandy-blond hair was shoulder length. His chest was chiseled and coated with a layer of blond hair that also covered his arms and legs. His face sported blond sideburns, and his chin was covered with flaxen hair.

I was stunned at how handsome and riveting he appeared but scared by his transformation. Then he snarled, and wolf fangs caught the light of the full moon.

Frightened, I retreated. "I have to go get help," I said.

I inched back, but he wasn't about to let me out of his sight. I felt like prey, the way he watched me, his eyes glued to me like he was a hunter.

Nash breathed heavily. And paced, slowly like a wolf—all the while his blue-gray gaze locked on me.

"It's okay," I said. "I'll be right back."

I wasn't sure if Nash knew who I was or what had just happened.

When Brandon had first transformed, he wasn't aware of what was going on. But Nash seemed to be stalking me. I continued to step back, not wanting to stay in the woods alone with him in this condition.

I wanted to run, but Nash was a star athlete on a good day. Now he'd be twice as fast. My only hope was to trick him. I started forward, then lurched back and ran. Nash had done this a million times, and I learned his fake-out from the football field. There was no way to outrun him, but I had to at least get a head start.

I screamed as I raced as fast as I could. The parking lot was far away, but the lake glistened only a few dozen yards from us. I was quaking as I tore down the hill.

I could feel his breath on my neck. I knew any minute he'd be on my back. It was only a few feet more to reach the lake when I felt his hand on my shoulder and I went down with a thud.

For a moment I was stunned. When I got my bearings, two blue-gray eyes were staring into mine. Nash was leaning over me, blocking me from getting up. He growled, bearing the fangs of a wolf. And I knew I was in danger.

He leaned farther into me and drew his fangs up the nape of my neck, sliding them up as if they were a knife. I didn't feel pain—just the threat of it. Then he took his finger and traced around my face.

I felt like he was checking me out. I wasn't sure if he knew that I was Celeste and that he was in fact a human, too. I wasn't ready to be his dinner.

As he locked his gaze on me again, I pried my foot between us and kicked against him with all my might. He fell back a few inches, which gave me enough space to slither out from his grasp.

I raced ahead and realized I was trapped by the lake. With no other alternative, I jumped in and swam for my life. When I got a moment, I looked back. Nash just stood at the edge and paced. I treaded water, waiting as the ripples calmed.

Nash peered into the moonlit water and saw his reflection. What he saw staring back startled him. He touched his face and arms. He looked around at the lake and then at me. His hunter's eyes softened.

I think then he realized what had happened, and his face filled with sorrow. Nash paused, as if in despair. Then he let out a maddening howl and tore off into the woods.

I waited for a few seconds but he didn't return. There was no one else in the park but me. I didn't have much time to escape. Dripping wet, my shoes filled with lake water, I raced back through the park. When I got to my car, I locked the doors and sobbed. I didn't know who to call—the police, Ivy, my parents, or Brandon.

I called Brandon, but he didn't answer. I hurried back

home, locked myself in my room, and was changing into dry clothes and softly crying when I heard a tapping at my window.

I was afraid to peer out. I knew Nash might be stalking me. When I heard a tap again, it took all my strength to be brave enough to pull back my curtain. What I saw surprised me.

A werewolf was indeed standing outside—but it was Brandon.

I ran downstairs, out the back door, and flew into his arms.

"I'm so glad to see you," I exclaimed.

"You are? But you weren't at the park. Are you okay?"

"You took the serum?" I asked, his wolf fangs shining at me. "It didn't work?"

"No," he said, caressing my hair. "I just didn't take it. I wanted one last night like this. I wanted to be cured, but then when I had the chance, I just froze."

"You want to be a werewolf?" I asked.

"I don't think so. But there was a part of me—I just figured one more night. But when I got to the park—you weren't there. The place was empty, but the scent of other wolves was there. I'm glad you didn't come."

"I did go. I was there—but so was Nash," I said.

"What was he doing there?"

"He wanted to apologize to me."

"Is that all?" he asked.

"Yes, but then the full moon came out and he changed! Nash changed!"

Brandon stepped back. "What?"

"He became a werewolf!"

Brandon's expression was severe. "Did he hurt you?"

"I think he wanted to. I was so scared—I'm not sure he knew what was going on. I felt so bad for him, but I was truly frightened—for him and for me."

"So did he attack you?"

"No, it was more like he was stalking me—like the wolf was doing to that deer the night Nash was bitten. He saw what he looked like in the lake's reflection. Then he took off."

"I should have been there for you," he said.

"There was no way to know for sure that this would happen—that he'd be there."

I was shaken up. I sat with Brandon beside a tree. He kissed and caressed me. I could feel his heart racing as he tried to calm me down.

"What do we do?" I asked.

"There is nothing we can do tonight," he insisted. "We can try to take our minds off of it for a while." He stroked my cheek with the back of his hand. It was extra soothing with the soft, thin layer of dark hair that wasn't there during the day. "Would you like to?"

"Yes," I agreed.

"We can have our date out here," he said. "Back behind the houses."

"I'd like that," I said. "With you, I'll feel safe."

We walked in the woods, holding hands. Brandon gently guided me over fallen branches and through rough terrain. When we were deep in the woods, Brandon perked up like he'd sensed something.

"What?" I asked as he stopped in his tracks.

All of a sudden we were joined by a pack of wolves.

I hid behind him. I was nervous, even though I knew I must be safe with Brandon here. It was hard for me to let down my guard—it was my instinct to fear them. But the wolves just looked to Brandon as if he was the alpha male.

Brandon tried to reassure me it was safe. He patted the leader of the pack and I watched, as I always did, in awe. A few minutes later, he took my hand again and we continued walking as the wolves followed close behind like a pet dog might around the yard. It was as magical an experience as I could have imagined. I had longed to do nature activities with my friends, who preferred walking in the mall to the woods or a park. Not only did I get to experience wonderful outdoorsy activities with Brandon, but when he was in were-wolf form they were truly extraordinary.

We eventually stopped by a massive tree, and Brandon drew me into him and kissed me with extra intensity. I leaned my head on his chest as the wolves lay at his feet. But as I felt his werewolf heart race, I knew that there was another one racing in some other woods as well. I gazed up at Brandon and he, too, was staring off, with a burden in his gray eyes that hadn't been there before.

Another werewolf was running around Legend's Run now. And though Brandon and I tried to make this date perfect, neither one of us could lose the concern we had for Nash and the ramifications that were caused by the bite under a full moon.

aftermath

Beware of a bite under a full moon. It will complicate your love life. I recalled Dr. Meadows's prediction when Ivy and I had visited her shop. I thought perhaps she'd been talking about me or Dr. Maddox, but it was in fact Nash whom the psychic was channeling. Dr. Meadows's prediction had been accurate again. And now that Nash had been bitten and become a werewolf, I feared for him, and it was sure to complicate matters for Brandon and me.

At school the next morning, we girls met Dylan and Jake outside the front steps of school.

"The baseball storage shed was trashed last night!" Jake said, having just come from the field.

"We don't know who got into it—or what," Dylan said.

"Well, maybe you won't be able to play, and then you can spend more time with us," Ivy said.

"I'm not kidding. Thousands of dollars in damages," Dylan said. "The coach was really upset."

"Perhaps you are being paid back for trashing Brandon's locker," Abby said.

"What?" Ivy asked, dumbfounded.

Abby went stone-cold silent.

"Jake didn't do that," Ivy shot back.

"Uh . . . maybe you should ask Jake," Abby said.

"You vandalized Brandon's stuff?" Ivy asked like a disappointed parent.

"Just the once . . ." he confessed. "I mean twice . . . if you include the Jeep."

"How could you?" Ivy asked. "You aren't a juvie! What were you thinking?"

"That maybe he could use a lesson to back off of you girls," Jake said.

"Well, that is just totally ignorant," Ivy scolded. "And you knew?" She glared at Abby.

"I saw some paint cans in Dylan's truck and he told me."

"Why didn't you tell me?" Ivy asked.

"He swore me to secrecy."

"So you are the friend who kept a secret from me that Dr. Meadows warned me about," Ivy said. "Wait, both of my best friends did that to me?"

"Do you think Brandon did this?" she asked gently. "To get back at you guys?"

"Maybe it was Dylan and Jake—" Abby said.

"Hey—we wouldn't trash our own stuff," Dylan said.

"It looks like an animal did it," Jake offered.

"We're going to have to replace a lot of this equipment," Dylan added. "Maybe someone was very angry he didn't make the team."

"I still think it was an animal," Jake said.

Just then Nash came down the steps and joined us.

"Wow—you look ragged out, man," Dylan said. "Late night?"

"You guys went out?" Abby asked.

I remained silent.

"You have a scratch on your arm," Dylan said to me. "What gives?"

"Were you out with Nash?" Abby whispered.

"No, I didn't go out with him," I finally said.

"Did you hear about the storage shed being trashed?" Dylan asked Nash.

"Yes," Nash said. "Animals, real animals."

"Well, the Moonlight Dance is tonight," Abby said.

"I can't wait," Ivy added. "It's going to be a blast."

"Yes, I can't, either," Nash said.

The gang was heading for their lockers when Nash

stopped me at the top of the stairs.

"I need to talk to you, Celeste, in private."

"I'll catch up with you," I called to Ivy and Abby, who were still at odds because of Abby's secrecy.

"Something happened last night," Nash said. "I have to tell someone—and I know you won't tell anyone, right?"

"If you don't want me to."

"I dreamed all night," he said. "It was horrible. But the worst of it was that when I woke up, I was in the woods behind the baseball field."

He looked to me for my reaction. When I wasn't totally shocked, he was surprised.

"What?" he asked.

"Oh . . . nothing. Go on."

"I don't know what's happened."

I didn't have the heart to tell my first crush—my first boyfriend—that last night I'd seen him turn into a werewolf.

"How did I get there—and why?" he asked. "And if I was there—I must have seen who trashed the storage shed—but I don't remember who I saw."

"It's okay—" I said, even though I knew it wasn't. If Brandon had a cure, then maybe it could be used for Nash as well. I'd just need time to find out.

"What happened to your arm?" he asked. "Did Brandon . . . ?"

No, it was you, I wanted to say. I wanted to tell him that he was the one who'd attacked me. But with the bell ringing and other students hanging around, now wasn't the time to confess what I'd witnessed and experienced the night before.

"Nash doesn't remember anything," I told Brandon as soon as I was able to catch him between classes. "The baseball storage shed was trashed and he doesn't think he did it. But I do."

"Why do you think so?"

"Because he said he woke up in the woods behind the school. He told me not to tell anyone—but I figured you'd understand. I'm really worried about him, Brandon. He doesn't know about last night. Or why he woke up in the woods. He doesn't even know that he chased me in Willow Park. I couldn't bear to tell him he did—or what he became. The dance is tonight," I said, my heart racing. "He doesn't know he's going to turn."

"Who is he going with?" Brandon asked.

"I don't know. Maybe Heidi Rosen? I know I'm going with you."

"I don't think he'll be going with anyone," he said. "He's going to turn, and then he's going to inhabit the woods all night."

"You think?"

"I know," he said. "But I'm not. I'm going to be just like

every other guy there—taking his girlfriend to the dance."

"So we don't need to do anything about Nash?"

"There's nothing to do," he said reassuringly. "At least not tonight. Let's cure me first. Then we'll be able to cure Nash."

EIGHTEEN

moonlight dance

Brandon planned to take his antidote at sunset, and we agreed to meet at the dance. I was so excited to dance with him through the night. This was to be our first time together in public. Our relationship wouldn't be a secret any longer.

When I walked in, I heard a whistle coming from one of the trees.

It was hard to see with the glare of the school lights. I peered closer and saw steely gray eyes shining through the brush.

"Brandon?" I asked, running over to him. "What are you doing out here?"

When I saw that he was only wearing jeans, I knew he either hadn't taken the antidote or that it had turned him into a werewolf permanently.

"Are you okay?" I asked.

"I can't go with you," he said. "I tried to—I planned on taking it. But I was afraid of being a werewolf all the time—and not being one at all. I'm so confused. Then when I changed, I realized it was too late. Now I can't let you walk in there with a werewolf."

I held him with all my might.

"All I wanted was one dance," he said. "Just to be close to you and see your dress and watch you—just to walk into school holding your hand, like any other boyfriend would do."

"Boyfriend?" I asked.

"Yes."

"So you are my boyfriend. For real?"

"Of course!"

We embraced, and I didn't ever want to let go.

"I can't walk in there looking like this," he lamented. "I have long hair and a goatee—things I didn't have an hour ago. And I don't have clothes."

"It is dark inside, isn't it?" I asked.

"Yes . . . but . . . I just wanted one dance, that was all."

"Then you'll have your dance," I declared. "Can you wait here?"

"Uh . . . sure."

I did my best to hurry back up the front steps in my heels. I rushed down the hallways passing formally dressed couples.

"Hi, Celeste," several couples said.

The speech and drama room was open, as Mrs. Feldman, the teacher, was in the gym chaperoning the dance. I made my way to the back of the room and grabbed a men's black overcoat and wing-tip dress shoes and hurried back out with them.

I got a few curious stares from students as I passed by and rushed out the front door to Brandon.

"Here," I said. "You can wear these."

He examined the clothes. "They don't look too bad, actually."

"Yes, we are lucky the drama department has a good budget."

Brandon held my shoulder for support as he put the shoes on. I helped him adjust the jacket and wiped off any lint I saw.

"If you don't smile too big or grin widely, they won't see your fangs."

"What about my hair?" he asked. "How can I explain that it grew six inches in a day?"

"Hm . . ." I thought. "Wait."

I dug into my purse and pulled out a tiny ponytail holder. I combed his wild hair with my fingers and twisted his luxuriously thick mane and wrapped the holder around it. I tucked the ponytail neatly into the back of his jacket.

Now we were able to attend the dance like any normal couple at Legend's Run.

We entered the Moonlight Dance. We walked through an arch of black and white balloons into the dimly lit gymnasium.

Most students were surprised to see Brandon and me together. Whispers and murmurs followed us as we continued to walk into the room.

Ivy and Abby were already dancing with their boyfriends. When they spotted us, they stopped and came over to greet us while their beaus went for refreshments.

"You look beautiful," Ivy said.

"So do you guys," I said.

"Hi, Brandon," Ivy said. "Your eyes look different in this light."

Brandon smiled back and greeted Ivy and Abby.

"Celeste is right, you girls look beautiful," he said.

Ivy and Abby blushed and giggled.

"So how long have you been here?" I asked.

"Not long," Ivy said.

"The DJ is great. You'll have to get out there," Abby told us.

"We plan to," Brandon said eagerly. "I was hoping to wait until a slow song," he said into my ear.

We hung out for a few minutes until the DJ played a slow tune, and Brandon led me onto the dance floor.

He pulled me close, and I wrapped my arms around his neck. I wasn't looking anywhere else or thinking about anything else. I was dancing with my romantic werewolf, and no one had any idea.

When we finished, Brandon gazed down at me like he'd done when we were hidden under the staircase, tucked away in his guesthouse, or nestled together in the woods. I felt as if he was going to kiss me—this time in front of the whole school. Then Brandon leaned into me and drew me closer and planted his lips on mine with the intensity of a thousand leading men. I was lost in his lips for what seemed like forever.

When we broke apart, I felt hundreds of staring eyeballs fixated on us. Ivy, Abby, Jake, Dylan, and every student gawked at us. Even the staff and chaperones were staring. Brandon was unaffected and just grabbed my hand and proudly led me off the dance floor.

When we joined my group, there were a few howls from the guys and gaping faces from my girlfriends.

Brandon smiled while I blushed.

The guys went to grab us girls a few drinks when I noticed Heidi Rosen walking in with one of the athletes—not Nash.

If Nash wasn't with Heidi and he wasn't here, where was he? I was hoping he was concealed in the woods like Brandon said he'd be. I was worried about Nash. He was probably somewhere in the woods hiding. However, until sunrise it was for the best. Once Brandon took the cure and we found it worked, then maybe Nash could as well.

The guys returned with our punch, and Brandon seemed preoccupied. "Thank you," he said to me as he handed me my drink. "I got my one dance."

"I don't want you to leave," I pleaded. But I didn't know how much longer it would be until someone noticed his paranormal characteristics. His hair was already becoming a little frazzled from dancing, and his goatee and facial hair could be seen when the flashing strobe light hit him at the right angle.

"I know, me too." As my clique sipped punch and gossiped, Brandon drew me aside and gave me a long goodnight kiss. Then he slipped out the side door without anyone the wiser.

"Where's Brandon?" Ivy asked.

"Uh . . . he wasn't feeling well."

"I can't believe Nash didn't come," Abby said. "Maybe he's sick, too."

There was a commotion coming from the gymnasium's entrance, and a startling howl came from that direction.

"What was that?" Ivy exclaimed.

Some students screamed while others stepped aside.

"There's a wolf in here!"

Then the lights came on. Everyone scrambled for the sides of the gym. But there wasn't a wolf in sight. Instead, Nash entered the gymnasium.

He was fully illuminated by the gym lights. His hair was wildly long, and he had sideburns and blond facial hair. His normally athletic body was even more ripped. He was wearing dress pants and nothing else. Nash was growling.

Several girls screamed at the sight of him.

"He looks like a werewolf!" one girl exclaimed.

"A gorgeous one!"

"Why does he look like that?" someone asked.

"He has wolf fangs!" another said.

"This has to be a joke!" Ivy said.

"He's pranking us again," Abby declared.

When Dylan headed for him, I called out, "Be careful, Dylan. He's not pranking."

"You mean to tell me—" Ivy started.

When Dylan reached Nash, he stared at his friend. Suddenly Dylan retreated and came back to our huddled group.

Nash headed straight for me.

"But what's he doing?" Ivy asked.

"He wants Celeste," someone said.

Nash grabbed me by the arm.

"Get off of her!" Abby said, trying to break me free. But Nash's grip was too tight for the ponytailed athlete. He pulled me to the dance floor. Everyone was shocked.

"You're hurting me!" I said.

Then Nash locked his blue-gray eyes on mine, and I was under a spell. He was magnificent, even more muscular than he normally was. His shoulder-length, untamed, beach-colored hair was beautiful.

He took me into his arms and held me so close I could feel his heart beating against mine.

"What's wrong with him?" I heard others whisper.

The music had stopped, but that didn't curtail Nash from beginning to dance with me as if it were still playing. He grinned, and his wolf fangs shone brightly.

I wasn't sure what he was going to do next. If he bit me, I suspected I would become a werewolf, too. He had his sights set on me, and I didn't know what to do. All I knew was that I was becoming frightened of him, and it seemed as if everyone else in the gymnasium was, too.

I didn't want to anger Nash any further for fear he might strike out at me—or someone else.

"Jake—do something," Ivy said.

"What can I do?" I heard him say. "He's just dancing with her."

"C'mon, Dylan!" Abby yelled. "She doesn't want to dance with him!"

"She seems okay," he said.

"Then I'll get her," I heard Abby say.

Just then Brandon entered the gymnasium. He was still wearing the outfit I'd given him. Only this time, the gym was fully illuminated. Brandon's hair was long and tousled, and his face was lined with hair. Fangs broke through the separation in his lips. Because the lights were on, everyone could see his lycan condition.

There were gasps and whispers and a few screams.

"What's going on?" Dylan asked.

"Call nine-one-one!" someone hollered.

"He's a—" Jake said.

Brandon stared straight at us, and his gray eyes bore through the gym right at Nash.

Nash perked up, as if he sensed a competitor on his turf. He turned us around so I was the one standing in front of him. Nash held on to me so tightly, there was no way for me to escape.

Brandon grew wildly angry, and he was primed for a fight. The moment was surreal, as if I were in a movie. Brandon charged the dance floor and with all his lycan strength pulled Nash away from me.

I fell to the ground, and Nash was thrown back off the dance floor but landed on his bare feet.

Ivy and Abby raced over and helped me up, quickly guiding me off the dance floor.

Nash jumped back into the middle of the gym floor and squared off with Brandon, as if at any moment one was going to charge the other.

Just then two security officers stormed into the gym. As the two werewolves were primed to lunge at each other, the officers headed toward them.

Nash let out a fierce howl that startled all the girls, causing screams and panic. Just before the officers reached him, he took off for the opposite gymnasium doors while Brandon headed to comfort me.

Nash busted open the fire exit door and ran off into the night, setting off the alarm.

Everyone covered their ears as the chaperones and security guards scrambled to find Brandon and Nash and to disable the alarm.

While the commotion was going on, Brandon grasped my hand and led me to the front entrance of the gym and outside into the darkness.

When we reached the edge of the woods and were safely

out of view, Brandon took me in his arms. "Are you okay?" he asked.

I was still shaken. The night had ended so strangely. My teeth were even chattering from nerves. Brandon held me like a little bird that had broken a wing.

"It's over now," he said.

"Is it?" I asked. "Now everyone knows. About Nash—and you." Brandon took off the jacket and placed it around me. I wasn't cold, but I was freaking out. His caring nature was the only thing that was going to calm me down.

He removed his shoes and T-shirt. He stood in front of me like the handsome werewolf I'd seen before.

"You are always saving me—and everyone," I said. "Who is going to save you?"

A smile overcame him, and he beamed like the moon above us.

"The one girl standing in front of me," he said. He drew me in his arms and I fell into his embrace. "By finishing our dances together underneath the moonlight."

magic of the moonlight

The following day, the town was abuzz with the Moonlight Dance fiasco. Apparently once the alarm was disabled, the dance continued, but not without much gossiping about the astonishing event. Ivy and Abby texted and called me after the dance, and I assured them I was okay and agreed we'd meet at the coffee shop in the afternoon.

Nash spotted me outside my house as I was heading over to catch up with my girlfriends.

Back in his human form, he looked disheveled and tired. Normally the handsome jock was pretty immaculate and clean in his preppy threads and gelled hair. But I found him at the end of my driveway in a T-shirt and jeans and with scratches on his arms and face.

"I don't know what happened last night," he said, almost shaking. "Everyone is looking at me strangely and calling me Wolf Boy. What's happening to me?"

I hadn't seen Nash this scared since he was attacked by the wolf in the park.

"I can't tell you now," I said. I was afraid to add more pain to him in his already anxious state.

"They are saying I'm a wolfman. Just like we teased Brandon. But I don't know why. Why me?" His torment was palpable.

"Where did you get those scratches?" I asked.

"I don't know," he said as truthfully as I'd ever heard him. "I need your help. You are the only one I feel safe with. You are the only one who really knows me—and can tell me what happened last night."

I patted him on the arm, hoping to comfort him. "Do you remember being at the dance at all?" I asked.

"I only remember getting ready. It got dark and I felt ill. Then I woke up outside my house. I guess I passed out from partying?" He looked to me for an answer, but even though he didn't remember, I knew he sensed he wasn't out partying.

"Please, Celeste. You have to help me. I'm not a bad guy. I need to know what is going on with me," he pleaded. "I'm afraid I might hurt someone."

That was a game changer. It was one thing to see my friend struggle with not knowing what was going on, but if he wasn't remembering what was happening, how could he control what he was doing? He was a far different werewolf than Brandon was, and that meant I had to keep not only the town safe but Nash as well.

There was only one solution to help Nash. He had to remember. Then he could decide what to do with his condition. And there was only one way for him to remember.

"You will have to meet me at Willow Park tonight," I instructed. "By the lake. You must promise. Just before sunset."

"Okay," he said. "I really appreciate this, Celeste."

He leaned in for a hug, and I gave him a warm one.

"It's the only way for you to remember," I said as he got back into his Beemer.

"Remember what?" he asked as he shut the door.

Ivy and Abby were already waiting for me at the coffee shop by the time I arrived.

"What is going on?" Ivy asked.

"Nash is a werewolf!" Abby said. "And so is Brandon."

"No they aren't. They both were pranking us!" Ivy said. "Why do you fall for everything?"

"Because it's true. I saw it with my own two eyes. And so did the whole school!"

Ivy was skeptical, like I'd been when I first saw Brandon. Since Nash spent most of his time pranking us and our schoolmates, it was reasonable to believe this was a prank, too. But Brandon? I wasn't sure what to tell my friends.

"Half the town agrees with me that it was a prank," Ivy said proudly.

"And the other half agrees with me," Abby argued. "We have werewolves in Legend's Run, and we saw two of them last night!"

I was disheartened. Even though I wasn't thirsty, I ordered some coffee to give myself something to distract me from my friends' conversation.

Abby turned to me. "Well, what do you think, Celeste? You were close enough to Brandon and Nash to see everything. Were they wearing makeup?"

"Uh . . . of course they were!" Ivy interjected.

"Let her answer," Abby insisted. "Were they, Celeste?"

Ivy huffed. "Leave her alone. The two guys were fighting over her last night. She's exhausted."

I was, but my day wasn't over. In fact it was only beginning.

"See, this is why I tried to tell you to date Eastsiders," Ivy lamented. "See how much trouble has happened? I have to know, Celeste. It may sound crazy. But I saw what I saw. And everyone is talking about it. Are you dating two werewolves?" she asked.

"No. I'm only dating one," I said.

They both were in shock and then began cracking up. And finally I, too, joined in. For the next hour we rehashed the bizarre events that had taken place last night, and for now my friends seemed keen on accepting those events of the Moonlight Dance as a prank.

It was late afternoon when I arrived at Brandon's house and found a car already parked in the driveway. Apollo was barking in the window.

A lady opened the car door, and it was then I noticed her long gray hair.

"Dr. Meadows—what are you doing here?" I asked, hopping out of my car.

"I'm friends with Officer Nichols," she whispered. "He told me what happened at the dance last night. He believed it to be a prank—but I knew better. Brandon is a werewolf."

I had enough on my plate without Dr. Meadows getting in the way of my helping Nash remember his transformation and curing Brandon's lycan condition.

"It's a full moon," she said. "I want to see what happens."

"You have to leave," I insisted. I was going to block her way if I had to.

Brandon stepped out of the house. "May I help you?" Brandon asked.

"I'm here to visit your grandparents," Dr. Meadows said. "But it is you I really wanted to talk to. I'm Dr. Meadows."

Brandon's face perked up. "Dr. Meadows?"

"Yes. I want to talk to you about a few things."

"I can't," he said. "Not tonight."

"Oh . . . but it must be tonight."

"We have a date," Brandon said.

"But this won't take long," she said, noticing the sun beginning to set.

"We really have to go—perhaps another time," I said. I pulled Brandon into my car and drove out of the driveway.

I peeked in the rearview mirror and noticed she was scrambling to get into her car.

"She wants to see you turn," I said.

"We can't let her."

"I know!"

I drove around a few bends and could tell she was following us.

"We have to lose her," I said. I felt like I was in an action movie. But in a movie, I had the safety of my couch or theater seat. Here, I was in the car, and I was the one driving.

"Just be careful," he said, looking out the back window. "Drive like you would normally and I'll tell you when to pull off. I know a few back roads."

I was scared to think that Dr. Meadows would see Brandon's transformation. If she had a camera or video, she would also have proof of the lycan event. It would change everything for Brandon if the town had proof he was a werewolf.

I continued to drive steadily, like I normally did, and tried to remain calm, but my hands were warm around the steering wheel. My nerves were getting the best of me.

"She's still there," I said, glancing in my rearview mirror.

"Yes," he said, "but she won't be for long."

"What are we going to do? Where are we going?"

"Just a minute . . ." he said. And then, "Now! Turn off here." He pointed to a gravel road.

I quickly made the turn.

"Now give it some gas!"

I pressed my foot on the accelerator, and dust from the road kicked up into a cloud behind us.

"I can't see her; is she there?" I asked as we raced on.

"No, she didn't follow us. But if she turns around, she might find us," he said. "We have to drive a little farther until we come to a fork."

It wasn't long before I saw the road splinter off into two directions like Brandon said it would. "Which way do we go?"

"The left one."

We headed onto another gravel road and found ourselves deep in the back country of Legend's Run. Eventually Brandon told me to stop.

"I've never done that before," I said, my heart pounding almost loud enough to hear.

"Hopefully we won't have to do it again."

"It was so exciting!" I tried to catch my breath.

The dust settled, and Dr. Meadows's car was nowhere in sight. "You are amazing!" I exclaimed. My friends barely knew the main road on the west side of town, so it was thrilling to know someone who only lived here a short time but knew his way around the back roads of the town I was born in.

"If we continue on, this road dumps out a half a mile from the park," Brandon told me.

I took a breath and continued driving. It was then I realized the other threat, the one we were originally dealing with today—Nash's transformation.

"Nash is going to hurt someone if he doesn't know what he is doing," I told Brandon. "You saw him at the dance. He doesn't remember his actions. I think he destroyed the baseball storage shed the first night he turned. You saw how he was at the dance—stalking and preying on me. He's not like you. It affects him differently. He becomes an untamed animal." I paused for a second and then told Brandon what I planned to do. "I think the only way that I can help him remember is to do what I did for you—to kiss him under the full moon."

With Nash not remembering the events that took place when he was a werewolf, it was up to me and Brandon to tell or not to tell him what happened. There was only one way to break the spell of not remembering—what Dr. Meadows had warned me against. Kissing a werewolf. I didn't want to do it—I wasn't dating him anymore, and it felt wrong to consider kissing him again. It wasn't like he wasn't the hottest Eastsider in school; it was just that I'd fallen in love with the hottest Westsider.

But Brandon wasn't so eager for me to trade my affections for Nash's benefit. "Are you kidding?"

"No," I said.

"I can't stand by and watch you kiss another guy."

"I'm not asking you to—"

"So you want me to leave you alone with him?"

"No . . . I just mean it's the only way to cure him from not remembering. And if I don't—you saw him last night."

"I know, I know." He looked away.

"But it'll tear me apart to know you're kissing another guy." He was forlorn, and I, too, felt awful.

"I'll make it quick," I said as he turned back to me. "It'll be like kissing a friend."

"I can't even think about it," he said with a snarl. "But if he remembers, he won't attack you again."

"That's what I hope," I said.

"But maybe I will," he teased.

We both laughed but knew that the situation was awkward, to say the least. The sooner we got there, the sooner I could help Nash and be back in Brandon's arms.

When we arrived at Willow Park, I checked in the rearview mirror and didn't see Dr. Meadows's car.

"We lost her for good," I said.

Brandon and I jogged to the lake, hoping to reach it before the sun fully set.

"You better make this quick," Brandon warned. "Just a peck. Like you'd kiss a friend."

"Okay, I promise," I said.

Brandon kissed me for a long time, and then stepped into the brush.

I found Nash leaning against a tree by the lake. The setting sun shimmered against the water. He almost seemed startled when he caught sight of me approaching. It was as if he was surprised that I showed up.

"I'm glad you came," he said, relieved. "I wasn't sure—"

"I know," I said. "I'm here."

"You really are the one person I can count on. You always have been. I really mean it, Celeste." He took my hand in his. "It's always been you. I guess I focused too much on myself and not enough on you. I don't know, maybe I didn't think we should be so serious, since we are still young. But I was wrong to do so. You've always been my best friend—and more than that . . . you are the only one for me. And you always will be."

His kind words were sincere, and I believed them. Nash was charming, but he wasn't dishonest. The fact that he now recognized what our problems were spoke volumes to me of how he was really changing in a mature way. But had I not met Brandon, Nash would still be talking about his scores instead of his love for me. And had I not met Brandon, I might still be dating the athletic Eastsider instead of being in love with the outdoorsy Westsider.

The sun set and the full moon lit up the sky behind him.

"I'm so hot!" Nash said suddenly.

He dropped my hand and began to rip off his shirt.

I knew what was happening, but that didn't make me any less afraid for him and the situation.

"I'm freaking boiling!" he exclaimed as he threw off his shoes and socks.

"I know," I said helplessly. "It will be okay."

Nash fell to his knees, and his eyes turned blue gray. He shuddered and managed to rise and stumble behind a tree.

Just then I heard the howling of two wolves.

Nash returned, his normally gelled, flaxen hair untamed and hanging to his shoulders. His blue-gray eyes bore through the darkness. He was attractive and muscular and had sexy sideburns and wild blond hair on his face and chest.

I still was slightly scared, but Brandon was only a few yards away if anything got out of hand.

I knew what I had to do. It was imperative that Nash not spend another night as a werewolf, not remembering his actions. But this was the same werewolf that had tried to attack me last night and the one before.

"Nash—" I said. "I need you to remain calm. It's just me, Celeste. Your best friend."

Nash remained by the tree and breathed heavily.

"I don't want you to hurt me," I said, my voice quivering. "And I know you don't want to. You want us to be together."

I inched toward my former boyfriend. He didn't retreat or charge me. Instead he appeared accepting.

I reached out my hand, and he growled. I did my best not to run or freak out. When he extended his hand to me, I felt slightly more comfortable.

I took his hand, which was warmer and stronger than

normal. I looked up at him under the moonlight like I had so many times when we were dating, but this time a werewolf stared back at me. So much guilt raced through me. First getting Brandon in this situation and now Nash. I was here to do something to try to ease the situation as best as I could.

Nash's hair hung in his face and on his shoulders. His blue-gray eyes softened as I continued to hold his hand. "It's okay," I said in a whisper. "I'm not going to run away tonight. It's the only way you'll remember."

Then I leaned in and he did the same.

I kissed him full on the mouth, our lips pressed together like they had many times before. His lips were even more riveting and tender than the kisses we'd shared when we were dating. But even though this kiss would be memorable, there was still something deep down inside me that was missing. He had been my first crush, but even in this powerful state, he still wasn't my first love. Tears welled in my eyes as I knew I felt as much for him as I could. And I was now ready for it to end.

I quickly pulled away to find Brandon standing next to me. His wolf eyes were intense and his fangs were shining. He was scowling angrily, and I wasn't sure what to do. Had I finally brought out the animal in Brandon, too? Maybe it hadn't been right to have kissed Nash. In Brandon's normal state, he might have dealt with it—but now he was alone in the woods with another werewolf, and perhaps I'd made a horrible mistake.

Instead of running to Brandon, I inched back. When he saw the fear in my eyes, his intense expression softened.

"It's over—" I said. "Now Nash will remember. And he'll remember I'm with you," I said, and raced into his arms.

Nash was dazed. He stumbled for a few seconds and then stared at both Brandon and me. Brandon then blocked me from Nash's view. But instead of challenging Brandon, Nash just smiled a huge, shifty smile, wolf fangs shimmering. He roared a wildly enthusiastic howl and tore off into the woods.

Brandon growled and turned around to face me. He gazed down like I was a small animal he wanted to protect. I leaned into Brandon, all the tension from my body caving into him. I would never stop caring for Nash. He was my friend and an attractive guy, to say the least, and I wanted the best for him. But I also wanted the best for me. And that meant being with Brandon.

"From now on," he said, staring down at me with his sexy gray eyes, "I'm the only one who's going to be kissing you."

Brandon swooped me up in his arms and passionately kissed me with the power of a hot, handsome, and heroic werewolf.

Even though I was happy, I knew Brandon and I still had our challenges ahead. There were two werewolves in Legend's Run now. I had dated one and was in love with the other. And with the high school witnessing both, I knew we all weren't out of the woods yet.

But for now, I enjoyed kissing the werewolf I was in love with, the magnetic one with irresistible lips, a howling heart, and superhuman strength, who loved me just as I loved him, among the trees and underneath the glow of the full moon.

ACKNOWLEDGMENTS

I'd like to thank these fangtastic people:
Katherine Tegen, Ellen Levine, and Sarah Shumway
My family, Dad, Mark, and Ben
My in-laws Jerry, Hatsy, Hank, Wendy, Emily, and Max
and my best friends, Linda and Indigo